Rampike

European P. Douglas

Published by Ghost Creative, 2018.

RAMPIKE

First edition. June 1, 2018.

Written by European P. Douglas.

Chapter 1

Deep orange glowed through the cracks in the blackened embers; the ash crumbling and shifting in the battered tin bowl as Maul Thorndean swivelled it around. Ever since he was a boy he'd loved to see the dying of the fire and listen to the last death of embers rattling around in the dented vessel. The bowl grew hot, and he had to shift it from hand to hand keeping his thick fingers in constant motion against their burning. His vapored breath in the cold air fused with the wisp from the ashes and he spat into the bowl to add a hiss to the effect. When he'd watched long enough, he tilted the bowl and let the embers fall, breaking to the hard earth at his feet.

Maul looked through the trees and saw the town of Emerson down in the valley, about ten miles away. It was the closest town to his own home of Mercy and yet not once in his forty-five years and six months had he been there. It looked much bigger than Mercy, but that wasn't saying much. With only one street and a few houses spread around the woods it was lucky it even had a name. Maul was sure that when he was a child, his father had never once even mentioned the name of Mercy and it was possible he didn't even know the name of the place he lived. The Thorndean's had been an isolated clan going back longer than Maul could remember; a tradition he was more than happy to continue.

It had been said in the past that Mercy only was named at all to justify having a sheriff who could keep tabs on the wild ways of the Thorndean's. It was fanciful but Maul wasn't sure that made it untrue. There was a sheriff after all; Joe Moorefield at the present time and he represented very, very few people.

A bright flash in the valley caught his eye and the telltale crack of the rifle shot came a moment later. The cries of a wounded animal, a young deer by the sound, rose pitifully on the sharp air.

"Not a great shot," Maul mused. The animals he killed never had the luxury of knowing their fate like that. He looked to his own kill from the morning, a hefty doe that would feed him for a few weeks to come. He'd sat to rest and recover some of his strength but it was time to get moving again. Standing up he grabbed the ropes that held the rim of the tarp in which he dragged his dressed meat and began to walk home, the ropes joining over his shoulder and pressing into the padding he wore there for this very reason. A mile behind him lay the rest of the carcass and he wondered if the wolves would have arrived there yet or would it still just be the birds pecking away at the meat.

A mile on from his fire site Maul took his first step back on to his own land; the most cherished and sacred thing in the world to him. It had been instilled in him from a young age that under no circumstances should he ever part with this land. This was the place where the Thorndean's belonged — the only place. It would take his death to remove Maul from the land.

As he waded through the thigh high grass, a cluster of thin trees to the south caught his eye. Something about them didn't look right but he couldn't tell what it was from where he stood. The trunks looked almost white in the morning light. He dropped the ropes to the ground and walked over to investigate. As he got closer, he saw that his eyes had not been deceiving him and the bark of the trees had turned white in large parts, looking like they had been scorched in a fire or struck by lightning long ago. It puzzled Maul as he knew for certain that this damage had not been here only two days ago when he had been chopping wood just by here. He felt the bark and found that it was smooth and hard with not a bobble to be found on the sections affected.

He wondered if it was the beginning of some kind of disease, like the Dutch Elm that had almost wiped out that species in these parts over fifteen years earlier. Maul looked around to see if he could see the marks on any other trees but nothing came to his eyes. It wouldn't be so bad to have some of the trees here die and fall eventually, but he was sure he didn't want them all getting a disease that might have the end effect of driving the animals out of the area, and with them his main source of food. He rubbed his hands on the smooth bark once more before going back for his meat and heading on home.

Maul's house was a large wooden structure that once served as a family home. It had four bedrooms and one central room that housed a rudimentary stove. He lived alone here and three rooms were almost completely neglected, the doors to them having remained shut for a very long time. On getting to the house he let go of the tarp and went inside, propping his gun against the wall just inside the door. He settled into a chair for a few moments and felt the stove for the heat left in it. Stoking the fire inside brought small flames, and he tossed light dry bark inside for kindling to get it started up again. It had been a cold morning and Maul felt much more weary than usual when he was out hunting. Though he'd slept well last night he thought if he lay down in bed he would find it very easy to fall back to sleep.

"You must be getting old," he said and smiled.

Maul woke with a start and looked about the room. There didn't seem to be anything that might have woken him but he was very surprised that he had fallen asleep all the same. The fire in the stove was almost completely dead now, so he hadn't even got that going properly before nodding off. Panic suddenly shocked through his body and he rushed to the door.

"Come on," he said. "Be my lucky day!" Sunlight blinded him momentarily as he came out into the day and for a moment he thought the worst had happened. As his eyes adjusted, however, and the black spot that obscured part of his vision receded he saw that his meat pack was still lying where he left it. Thankfully there had been no carnivore out and about in the vicinity who felt brave enough to approach the house to take it. Maul sighed. That would have been a bad end to a long morning's work. He didn't know what had made him fall asleep like that but he knew he couldn't make a stupid mistake like that again. These weren't known as the Wolf Woods for nothing.

Not long after when the meat he would not use in the next few days was salted and hanging in the meat shed, Maul looked at the low level in the salt bag. He would have to go to town and get resupplied, a thought that brought a scowl to his face. He hated going there, and he knew it was somewhere he was not welcome, but he had no other way of getting salt to preserve his meat. That big woman at the tavern (he may never have known her name, but it wasn't coming to him now) was the only one who would take barter for the salt. The old prick in the general and grocery store only wanted cash, and that was something Maul had no access to. He had never had a penny in his entire life and he didn't see that he ever would. There had been trouble the first time his barter had been refused and sheriff Oakes — the one before this new guy— had pulled his gun and made Maul leave town there and then.

"I better take an inventory of everything I need," he said bitterly. "I don't want to have to go again for as long as I can avoid it." His voice had broken a general silence in the area but no sooner had he spoken than in the far distance a clipped thwacking noise started up — an axe chopping wood somewhere closer to town.

Maul looked in the direction the sound came from; he knew who it was, not his name, but he'd seen him in the forest before. His axe fell rhythmically and strong and he was good at it. Maul had watched him once from the crest of a rise when the man didn't even know he was there. To Maul, the man looked like he had something else on his mind when he chopped, like he was burning off energy or perhaps even anger in a way that affected no one else. Of all the people in the area, this was the only one who did not seem to annoy him and for whom Maul had even the slightest modicum of respect. He listened to the chopping a few more moments and then went about his business.

One hour later Maul entered the tiny town of Mercy. He'd approached the town from higher up the slopes of the mountain and he stopped in the middle of the street and looked down. So many trees had been cleared to make way for the town that there was a clear view from here to Emerson and beyond that, more miles distant, some other town that Maul had never even bothered to find out the name of.

As he looked down on Mercy, his eyes met the first person of his visit. Mouse Allen looked at him from the door of the general store, his mistrustful eyes beady and narrow on him.

"What the fuck are you lookin' at fatso?" Maul called to him. For a moment, Mouse didn't answer and Maul could feel him squirming. The man was huge and probably stronger than Maul was but though he prided himself on his manliness, he had none of the wildness in him that made Maul such an unwelcome physical opponent.

"You don't get to talk to me like that you crazy asshole," Mouse said. Maul noticed that the big man didn't make any move closer to him but stayed stood where he was. Maul took a few steps closer himself instead.

"I can talk to anyone just as I please, fatso, and no one is going to do anything to change that!" he said pointing a finger towards Mouse.

"I'm not fat, you idiot!" Mouse said angrily, but he came off sounding like a wounded child.

"You'd feed a family of ten for a long time if you were roasted," Maul said and looked past Mouse towards the tavern which was his destination today.

"One of these days Maul, I'm gonna make you sorry for the way you treat people around here," Mouse said. Maul looked at him and saw that his fists were balled and his teeth clenched so tight that white lines showed across his blazing red cheeks.

"Why not today?" Maul asked with a malicious sneer. He dropped the bag he was carrying and stepped another foot towards Mouse with his arms outstretched as though inviting the first punch. Mouse glared back at him but still made no move. Maul could see the hatred in the man's eyes but more importantly, he could see the fear that was in them too. His father had told him many times growing up that if you see fear in an opponent's eyes the fight was already won.

A man appeared in the doorway of the store and put a hand on Mouse's arm,

"Best not to get involved, eh?" the man said. Mouse continued to look at Maul a few moments longer and then he looked to the man who had come out of the store. He nodded,

"I guess so, Jeff." Jeff nodded his approval and went back into the store without so much as looking at Maul. Mouse took one more look at the mountain man and shaking his head followed Jeff inside. Maul smiled at the space where Mouse had been. It was probably best there was no trouble before he got his business completed; he didn't want to be run off with nothing to show for the long walk down here. He picked up his bag and went on down to the tavern.

The door was open, but no one was inside when Maul entered the warm building. Two large logs white hot with glowing centres showing through fissures in each lay smouldering in the fireplace and the large open room was cosy. It looked like a very nice place to sit and rest and have a beer and for a moment, he wished he could come here more often.

"Anyone here?" he called out.

"Be with you in a minute," a female voice came back from another room. Maul was glad it was the woman, and he walked closer to the bar and leaned on it while he waited. There were animal heads mounted on the wall all around the room and he assumed they had been brought in by the customers over the years. Probably all easy kills, he mused. At one point, there were so many animals on this mountain that you could shoot out your front door and hit something. That was all different now though; hence his long hiking hunts when he needed to replenish his meat stocks. Maul didn't know why there were so few hunting animals around anymore; he doubted anyone in town ever caught one these days.

The woman came out from a door behind the bar and he turned to face her.

"Maul Thorndean," she said with a smile he wasn't sure was genuine. She didn't look surprised to see him but then this was a formidable woman and Maul thought her more like a man than some of the men in town.

"I've come hoping to trade meat for salt and some bottles of beer," he said getting straight to the point. The woman looked at him for a moment and didn't reply. Maul was about to repeat what he'd said when she moved to the tap and pulled a glass of beer. He watched as she did this and then she put the full glass down on the bar in front of him. He looked at her with suspicion.

"I don't have any money," he said.

"I know," she answered, "Drink it up all the same and let me see what you have in that bag."

Maul heaved his bag up on the bar and took hold of the drink like this was the trade itself. He took a few large swallows, and it was all gone before the woman had looked properly through the bag. She looked at the glass and then at Maul with a playful expression.

"You want another one?" she asked. He did, but he didn't want to be in her debt.

"No," he said as mildly as he knew how. She leaned on the bar and looked at him for a long time. Maul, not one to be made feel uncomfortable stared right back at her. She hadn't done this to him before and he wondered was this some new bartering trick she had picked up and was trying out on him.

"You don't know what my name is, do you?" she asked breaking the silence.

"No, I don't," he answered without missing a heartbeat. She laughed out loud at this, throwing her head back and clapping her hands together once loudly.

"You're a character, Maul Thorndean," she said and then leaning on her side of the bar added, "I'm Sally Briers, pleased to meet you." Maul looked down at her outstretched hand but didn't take it.

"Are we trading or not?" he asked. He wasn't annoyed exactly, but he was confused by her behaviour.

"I guess I can give you what you need," she said withdrawing the hand without offence, her face still smiling.

"Good, and then I can get out of your town," he said.

"I don't have any desire to see you leave Maul," she said. "I wish you were here more often, you're the most interesting thing about this godforsaken town!"

"Pah!" he said waving this off. "I'd be dead up in my house for a year before anyone would think to come and look for me!"

Chapter 2

Maul wasn't gone all that long when the door to the tavern opened again and Sally looked up to see Mouse Allen and Jeff Sorkin come in. Sally looked to her watch and then back to the men.

"Early for you fella's aint it?" she said.

"Just popping in for a sandwich," Jeff said.

"And a beer," Mouse added. Jeff looked at him as in surprise but said nothing.

"I got some really fresh meat if you want me to fry some up?" Sally asked as she set to pouring the beers and the men took up a table in the centre of the room.

"Just your regular stock will be fine," Mouse said and there was an edge to his voice that didn't please her at all.

"What's eating you?" she asked him looking at him with steely eyes. Mouse didn't answer nor look in her direction. Jeff looked at him and sighed.

"I think—"

"I don' want to know what you think, Jeff," Sally interrupted him, "I want Mouse to answer me!"

"You know what's wrong with me," Mouse said sourly. "Or else you're dumb as an ass."

"I must be dumb as an ass then, cos I don't know what the hell you're keening over!"

"I'm not keening!" Mouse retorted and for the second time that morning sounded like a child being teased.

"Well then what is it? Spit it out!" Sally insisted, her hands on her hips waiting for his answer.

"What are you doing trading with that old fuck?" Mouse asked.

"Maul?" Sally asked to annoy Mouse more.

"Who else would I be talking about!" he cried out in exasperation.

"Why shouldn't I trade with him?" she asked.

"Because he's a mean spirited animal who might kill you as quick as look at you!"

Sally laughed aloud at this reaction and then even more so when she saw Mouse's face collapse in surprise at her not taking him seriously. Jeff put a hand on Mouse's arm that stayed him from saying whatever he was about to say at the moment.

"Maul is no more dangerous than any of you animals around here," Sally said. "He brings in good fresh meat too, which is much better than anything I get from the butcher in Emerson."

"He should stay up where he lives and not come to bother the rest of us decent people," Mouse said in a sulk and then looking to Jeff said, "You agree don't you?" Jeff nodded and then looked to Sally himself,

"He only comes here at all because you trade with him, Sally. You know what he's like don't you?" His voice was plaintive and he looked tired. Sally knew Jeff had been in a scrape with Maul before but it had been a long time ago now and she'd never had any trouble with the man. She felt sorry for him living alone way in the hills as he did. What kind of a life could he possibly have?

"I don't have a problem with him," she said. Jeff looked to Mouse and shrugged.

"Someone needs to put the man in his grave," Mouse said bitterly.

"Why don't you try it Mouse?" Sally asked.

"If Oakes was still sheriff around here I might!" Mouse said. "But this new fella would have the law on me in no time flat."

"Joe's been here a good while now," Sally said of the sheriff, "and he is the law himself."

"He doesn't have Mercy's best interests at heart; if he did, he would have sorted Maul himself."

"Well, at least that should be the end of Thorndean for a few more months," Jeff said settling back in his seat with his drink in hand. Mouse was scowling at his own glass and Sally, who knew the hot tempers of these isolated men, felt this was as good a place as any to rest the conversation about Maul Thorndean. She went to the galley kitchen and started on the sandwiches for the two customers; while frying a little of one of Maul's steaks to let them get a whiff of what they were missing.

The afternoon was quiet, as ever in the Lone Wolf Tavern, and Sally had plenty of time to her thoughts. Customers would come in one at a time throughout the day, sometimes overlapping with someone else but most times not. They would eat something, have coffee or some just a quick drink to warm the blood before going out to work in the woods. There had been a working silver mine in the area until about forty years previously and she could only imagine how much money former owners of this tavern must have made back then.

As she thought of the mine, she looked absently out the window at the rear of the building to the slopes where the mine opening had been. She could just about make out where it was, but it was all overgrown now and long neglected. The wood and trees around it looked pale and dead and she doubted anyone had been near it in years.

That evening the place filled around 8pm just as true dark was falling. Full to her tavern was at least one person at each table and one at the bar but it was enough for her to cover her small costs in running the place. Sally had bought it with money left in his will from her late father, a man who mined here and always felt he had left his heart in these mountains. She wanted to be where he would be most happy to find her and she also hoped that she could lose her heart to the place in the same way. It hadn't happened so far, but she had no plans to leave just yet.

By 9pm, all Sally expected to be in were there, including Mouse, who was one of those men who had the ability to completely forget any ills he might have had with a person in a matter of hours, unless that person was Maul Thorndean. He sat smiling at the bar talking to everyone as ever. The mood was jolly but Sally knew all it would take was one mention of the afternoon to change that. And so it was inevitable that someone mentioned it.

"I hear Maul Thorndean was down today?" Sam Brainard said with a smile from his corner table. He wasn't addressing anyone in particular but Mouse answered him.

"He was, more's the pity."

"Any trouble out of him?" Sam asked.

"None," Sally said before Mouse could answer. "Same as ever."

"I was out chopping near his land earlier today," Sam said. "Best not to think about how he feels about it. I guess he'd come and let me know if he had a problem."

"Be sure he would," Jeff said. He was at the bar beside Mouse.

"You're just sore he vented his spleen at you that time you wouldn't sell him anything," Alan Carey laughed from his table by the door.

"He had nothing to buy with!" Jeff almost screeched in his defence.

"Poor man, not a penny to his name and you wouldn't do the decent Christian thing and help a man out?" Alan was joking with Jeff and the two had had this conversation in the past but still Jeff was riled by it every time.

"I don't see you bringing up warm clothes and food from your own home to give to him," he said back hotly.

"I like to do my charity work out of the public eye," Alan said smiling like a benign priest.

"Yeah, so far out of the public eye, you don't even see it yourself, I bet," Mouse grinned.

"If you were all as generous to Maul as you are to me with tips, he would have been dead long ago!" Sally said with a loud laugh.

"We've tipped you generously with our wit and conversation over all these years," Alan said with a wink to his fellows.

"And for that I can only apologise," Sam said standing up as if to leave. He took some coins from his pocket and set them down by his glass and took his coat.

"You've no need to apologise, Sam, I've yet to take up your empty glass without finding you've left a little something," Sally said, and she was genuinely appreciative. He was a nice young man, and she was very fond of him.

"You leaving already?" Mouse asked Sam.

"Yeah, my back is aching and I need an early night tonight to sleep off the day's axe-swinging," Sam said.

"You won't have one more?" Alan said. "I can't be left with only this riff—raff." He motioned to the room.

"Why don't you head on home too if it bothers you," Jeff said without turning to look at him and Alan winked at Sally and Sam.

"I think I'll hang on until just about the time you're leaving Jeff and I can walk down the hill with you. You might even see me home, but no kissing mind!" The look of mirth on Alan's face was like that of a beaming child, and the others in the tavern couldn't help but smile along with him. All that was, save Jeff Sorkin, who was suddenly very affronted by the sexual slur he perceived in what Alan had said.

"You calling me queer!" Jeff said getting up and making for Alan with a ferocity no one there thought him capable of. Mouse grabbed him and Sally went to block his path as Sam leaned over the table that separated him from Jeff to try to add to slowing him down.

"Hey, hey, take it easy, Jeff," Alan said, "We're only having some fun here!"

"Come now boys," Sally said. "It's only fun if everyone is having fun."

"I'm sick of his shit," Jeff said, he was very upset, more so than Sally had ever recalled seeing him.

"I was only joshing," Alan said sounded wounded.

"Come on, Jeff, he was only playing around," Sam said.

"This is none of your business," Jeff said back snapping his head to look at Sam like he'd hit him. Sam held his hands in the air,

"Fair enough, I'm just trying to keep the peace."

"Sit down, Jeff," Mouse said. "Alan will get you your next drink." Jeff looked back at Alan who nodded in agreement. Jeff was breathing heavily as he resumed his seat and it took a few moments for him to settle.

"Get him what he wants, Sal," Alan said. "And everyone else too for that matter," he added. The place was silent now.

"I won't be serving anything unless you boys all cheer up," Sally said trying to infuse some life back into the evening.

"OK," Mouse said after another moments quiet. "What say we bust out the cards and get a game going?"

"I could go for that," Jeff said, and he looked over to Alan. "You?"

"You bet," Alan said with a slight smile and Sally knew that was the end of it. She never ceased to wonder at the way men would flare up and fight like that and then be friends only moments later even if it had come to blows. She shook her head in puzzlement for not the first time at these customer of hers.

"No gambling with real money," Sally said, and she took up the glass and money at Sam's vacated table.

"Imaginary money only," Mouse assured her.

"We can't tempt you to a game, Sam?" Alan asked. Sam smiled and went to the door shaking his head,

"I don't even have imaginary money to gamble with," he said and waving once went out into the cool night for his walk home.

The men mumbled a collective goodbye as they moved to the table in the centre of the room where the game would take place and Sally went to the bar to pull the drinks and go on living in the same way she did every other day in the small town of Mercy.

Chapter 3

For weeks now the white Maul had first noticed on the small cluster of trees had spread across his land. It had not only spread but new unaffected areas changed in the same way and it was coming in from three sides of his land and spreading outwards in a fan into the forest. He still did not understand what it was, but he was surer than ever now that it was some disease that was killing the trees. The speed at which it was happening was alarming — in only three weeks a third of his trees now showed the scarring and most of these were dead already.

Maul had never seen anything like it before and had no idea what to do about it. There was no one in town he could ask, not that he would anyway, and no memory or knowledge from his father to think back on. He took up his keenest axe and went outside to a part of his land where the trees had died recently. He felt the bark and looked at the trunk and limbs, taking a twig in his hand and napping it with ease, the loud crack reverberating in the forest. Leaning back, his took aim and let the heavy steel head thwack into the tree. The trunk shattered and splintered under the blow, and thousands of loud creaked followed straight away as the tree began to fall down, taking some its neighbours with it. Maul jumped back, dropping his axe in surprise and moved clear of the falling trunks.

The whole seemed to crash around him for a moment — the sound was louder than any tree felling he'd ever heard, and somehow far more terrifying. It was as though the wood itself was crying out in pain before being silenced with the thud on the hard ground. Birds flapped and jakkered in the air, angry from being disturbed and frightened at the same time. Bit of twigs, branches, bark and dust flew about the air and Maul covered his face against the wave that came at him.

When it all cleared, he stood there stunned.

"Holy fuck," he said absently. Never in his life had he seen a thing like this. The trees had broken like they were hollow porcelain vases. Maul leaned and looked at a part of trunk that lay nearest him. He picked it up and was surprised by the lightness. Turning it over in his hands, he saw that it was not hollow. The wood and rings were there all the way through and in fact inside it looked rather healthy. It was too light, however, that was the giveaway apart from the look of the bark.

The birds had settled now, and all was calm. Maul surveyed the new landscape; seven trees in all had fallen and two more were leaning perilously. He'd probably have to finish knocking them down, so it happened on his terms. He looked around the ground for the axe but didn't see it immediately. Kicking at some of the bark and twigs he came across the handle. As he bent to pick it up, he saw something that stayed his hand. The part of the handle visible to him was white, just as the trees had been. His mind didn't comprehend how this could be possible. He could understand a disease spreading from one living tree to another, but this was a long dead piece of wood, the handle for a tool for many years by now. It was impossible it could attract the same disease as the trees and yet this was exactly what he was looking at.

A breeze filtered over the ground then and Maul's incredulity was stretched even more when he saw that white was spreading over the rest of the axe handle right before his very eyes. Understanding came just as quickly when he realised it was the dust and debris from the crashing trees that lay over the handle and the wind moved some it off. He chuckled nervously at his own strange fear of the moment before. Composing himself he reached down and took up the axe.

By the time he had picked his path across the destruction to the first of the leaning trees he saw that there was no need for the axe at all. He pushed on the trunk and it fell easily, making that same crashing howling noise as before. The second one gave just as easily and soon all was quiet again. Maul looked around and couldn't stop the idea that soon enough there would no trees left at all on his land. There was no stopping this thing, whatever it was.

As he stood there surveying the ground the clacking noise to the chopping came to his ears. Without knowing he was doing it, Maul looked in the direction of the sound. He wondered if that young man was doing the same thing he'd been doing himself, trying to stop the infection spreading. The idea passed, and he didn't think so. Maul had made his way to the top not all that long ago and had been making a conscious effort to look at the trees on his way as he went. He'd been out scouting for animals too and had been mindful of them too and had found no evidence of anything wrong with the plant—life anywhere else.

Another thought, perhaps more pressing came to mind — it was possible this man who worked with trees all day might know how to combat what was happening on Maul's land. Approaching anyone from town was unpleasant to say the least, but he guessed he was in dire straits now and this was as good a solution, or possible solution, he would be able to come up with. If that young man didn't know what to do, then Maul didn't see he wouldn't have any options left at all. Thinking no more on it, he set off following his ears in search of the chopper.

It was close on forty—five minutes when Maul came across the man. Maul watched him for a few moments, taking him in as though he may need to fight this man — this was something was so ingrained in him he wasn't even aware that he did it anymore. The man was young, only his twenties. He was tall and thin but his frame must have held more strength that it looked capable of based on the divots made in the trees when he landed his blows with the axe. His swing was graceful and level and there was a skill in it that Maul could appreciate. He found that he had drifted into watching and a couple of minutes later shook his head like clearing it of a hideous thought.

"You know much about trees apart from how to hit them with an axe?" Maul called down between blows. The man's next crack was off and the axe shuddered in his hand and a noise other than sweet contact lilted over the forest.

"Fuck!" the man said letting his axe fall and rubbing one sore hand with the other. He looked over at Maul with a sour puss on him. "You couldn't have come closer to ask?"

"I figured you would be able to hear me fine from here," Maul answered, not put out at all by the man's annoyed tone. The man nodded his head at the blunt logic.

"I guess I do," he conceded, and a smile stole the corners of his mouth.

"So do you know anything about trees or not?" Maul asked.

"A little, what kind of information are you looking for?"

"I think I got a disease on the trees on my land."

"Dutch Elm?" the man asked.

"No, no elms left up there," Maul said, "Something white growing on the bark and the tree dies in days and its spreading like wildfire." The man thought about this a moment looking at the ground and biting his lower lip in concentration. Then he shook his head.

"Not anything I can think off hand," he said. "I'll be happy to go up and have a look with you?" Maul nodded at this and stood there. "You mean now?" the man asked and Maul nodded again.

"Now is when it's happening," he said.

"Fair enough," the man said, and he took up his axe and bag and walked up to Maul.

"I'm Sam Brainard, by the way," he said when he got to him. Maul took the outstretched hand and pumped it once, this man was doing him a favour after all, and then started walking back home.

Sam tried starting many conversations on the way but the best he could get out of Maul was the odd grunt and a couple of nods or shakes of the head. Maul didn't have any need nor want of chit—chat; he just wanted to know if he would lose his trees and if so how long before the whole mountainside was dead.

At last, they came to the first of the trees showing signs of the disease. They were not on Maul's land yet but it was within distance now.

"This is it," he said stopping so abruptly that Sam almost walked into the back of him. Sam looked at the tree and then putting his gear down ran his hands on the bark. He looked a little confused and then Maul could see there was something he wanted to say but he didn't quite know how to say it.

"Spit it out, boy," Maul snapped to spur him on.

"This looks like it was burned or hit by lightning or something a long time ago," Sam said almost apologetically. "I don't think this is anything recent."

"I know what it looks like!" Maul said indignantly. "It's not old though, this has all happened over the last few weeks."

"All of it?" Sam asked doubtfully.

"Every fuckin' tree!" Maul said. It didn't look like this young fella would know anything at all.

"I've never seen anything like this, but I have a lot of books at home. I can look and see if I can find anything out." Maul let Sam's words linger in his mind for a moment.

"So you don't have any suggestions?" Maul asked looking out over the trees.

"Not really," Sam said. "Other than the obvious."

"What's the obvious?"

"Containment." Maul looked at him still not sure what he was getting at. Sam took a moment to notice this and then added, "If you cut a gap between the sick trees and the healthy ones, that might stop it."

"Depending on how it's spreading," Maul said. Sam nodded,

"Yes." They stood a moment and looked around at the trees.

"I cut one down on my land but it broke on the impact of the axe and seven trees around it came down and broke up as well," Maul said.

"Broke up?"

"Looked healthy enough on the inside but much weaker than it should have been," he handed the wood he'd forgotten he'd was carrying to Sam. Turning it over in his hands, he felt the heft and ran his fingers through the grain.

"It feels light," Sam said.

"No strength left it in either," Maul added. Sam handed the piece back after a few moments and Maul looked at it once and then tossed it to the ground. "No use to me now."

"Like I say, when I get home this afternoon I'll have a look through my books and see if I can find anything," Sam said.

"I'd appreciate it," Maul said. The anger he was feeling was letting go to despair, and he saw his life going away from him.

"How much of your land is affected?" Sam asked just as he was about to leave.

"All of it," Maul said.

"You thinking you might need to move?" It had been said in innocence but Maul only heard the idea behind the words — the leaving of his land. He lunged forward and grabbed Sam by the shirtfront,

"I'll never give up that land!" he shouted into the younger man's stunned face. A wild idea raged in Maul's mind. "Did someone do this me?" he asked.

"What are you talking about?" Sam asked reeling on the slope and trying to get his footing.

"Did someone give this disease to my trees on purpose?"

"What?"

"Tell me the truth!" Maul roared, and he pushed at Sam and lost grip on his shirt. Sam stumbled backwards a few feet before losing his balance and falling head over heels down the hill ending up about twenty feet below Maul.

"You're fucking crazy!" Sam shouted back at him as he scrambled to his feet, expecting the wild man to bear down on him. Maul stood there looking down at him an urge to do violence abating since seeing him fall down the incline. "No one is out to get you!" Sam shouted at him before turning his back and walking away.

Maul stood there for a long time, long after he could no longer see Sam. It wasn't Sam's fault, he admitted, but the thought lingered that someone might have done this to his land. Hadn't his father told him from the day he could listen that this town wanted them gone? That was the way of things around here, and he supposed he had no reason to think it had ever changed. No matter what had happened, the trees on his land were almost all dead and soon the rest of the forest would go the same way. His life was changing and there was nothing he could do about it.

Chapter 4

Another week passed and Maul Thorndean was not surprised to find there had been no visit from Sam Brainard with news of the disease afflicting the trees. It was a lost cause now as far as he could see. The only chance was that the disease would run out of steam or the remaining trees might be able to grow some tolerance to it and push back. It was looking doubtful but Maul knew it was not impossible. In the meantime, all he could do was go on living as before and hope.

One morning he went hunting for something to pass the time and take his mind from the problem. He went far from his own land, and even his own usual hunting grounds and ended up close to the old mine entrance. The wooden beams that closed it off looked worn and rotten and he could see that some kind of animal had made a hole in it and was probably living inside. Maul could only imagine how many creatures might use such a thing as this disused mine shaft as a home. If he really wanted to all he would have to do was to wait a little distance off and shoot whatever came out. There was no sport in that, however, and even less to take his mind from his problems.

From where he stood now, he could see down on the town, the few building spread around. It was cold today and there didn't seem to be anyone around down there. Maul found it hard to see through the trees properly but he felt he could see the back of the tavern. He'd like to go down there and have a drink but knew this wasn't an option. He never ceased to have trouble in that town and if alcohol was thrown into the mix, he could end up killing one of them idiots down there. A vicious thought came to him just then — what did it matter if he did? There was nothing to hold his hand here now if his land and ability to find food would soon disappear.

The thought of doing harm to the people of Mercy sent a surge of power through him that took him utterly unexpectedly. Before he knew what he was doing, his hands, like acting independently of his brain, lifted the rifle and he aimed down at the street below. Still no one was in sight and he had to wonder if someone had appeared would his body have acted without him and pulled the trigger? His whole body was shaking in anger and he found that he was hoping someone would appear so he could find out. Something rattled in the low brush nearby but he didn't look to see what it was.

A new feeling came over Maul then, something that felt like slime on his skeleton. It was sickening, and he felt sweat on his brow. It was the feeling of eyes on him, someone watching him, and this was something that Maul didn't like at all. He scanned below and looked for the person he knew was observing him. His grip on the gun firmed up and his finger touched lightly on the trigger.

"Where are you fucker!" he whispered harshly. His blood was close to boiling now, and he knew he would take the shot if the target presented. His mind was clouding over, what the hell did it matter what he did now! He wanted it to be Mouse Allen or the prick from the general store; that would be worth it. Joe Moorefield would come for him then but that didn't mean Maul had to make it easy for him. He had enough ammo and dried meat to set himself up at home for a good time yet to come if it came to that. There was no way Maul Thorndean was going out without a fight!

His arms dropped suddenly when he did finally find the eyes of his watcher. They were sardonic and mocking but in a way Maul knew wasn't meant for him specifically. The woman, what had she said her name was? Sally? Was looking at him through the rear window of the tavern. She smiled when she knew he was looking back and then gave a military style salute. Maul didn't know how to react and he looked away and then turned and walked back the way he'd come. He was completely unnerved by her and he had no idea why. His anger had been raging, and he was seeking a target; she was the only person in town who could have stayed his hand. She was the only one who had never been anything but nice to him.

Maul didn't stop moving until he got back to his land. He almost felt like he was being pursued somehow, but he knew that was ridiculous. Still, it didn't stop him from looking behind himself from time to time just to be sure. He moved fast through the trees and never before had the need to be on his land been so strong in him. It made no sense but he could feel it burning within him that he had to get home and the sooner the better. He was so preoccupied that he wasn't watching where his going with his usual intensity and he turned once into a thick protruding branch that sliced into his cheek and stopped his dead in his tracks.

"Fuck!" he shouted as his hand went to his face. The branch was still stuck in his skin and he could feel the slick of his blood on his hands as he pulled it out. It had been very close to stabbing directly into his eye. It was painful, and he felt a thin flap of skin folded over as he rubbed at it. His anger rose again, but it directed at himself this time; he was fully aware this had been his own doing. His own stupidity and... what... superstition? Was that what it could be called, this running home and need to be safe there for no good reason he could discern. He tried to roll the skin back to where it belonged but fresh pain sprang up and when he let go it flipped over again. He pressed his hand to it and went on, meaning to see what he could do with the piece of mirror glass that was lying around in one of the rooms there.

By the time he got to his home, the bleeding had eased off, and the pain was like a dull throb but not too pressing. The area around the cut felt numb but stung viciously when he touched it. The grimy glass showed that he would be scarred by this but that didn't bother him all that much — his whole body was covered with nicks and cuts that had never healed, this was just the first time that one had been on his face.

"You won't win a wife, now," he said and smiled but as he spoke a pang of regret came over him for he knew that this was true. Not that he had ever wanted a wife, but he was very aware that he was the last of the Thorndean's and that the family name would end with him. And that end was looking more likely than ever before.

Maul forced himself to look back in the mirror. He took some water and washed the cut as best he could with his washing cloth. It hurt, but it was lessening all the time and he was sure it would be fine in a day or two. When he was done, he wiped the surface of the mirror to take off the dusted grime that had accumulated since it was last touched. It sparkled in the light and he knew that he should have done this before he used it to look at his cut. It didn't matter now, and if it was ever used again, it would probably be covered in the neglect of dust and grime just as before, anyway.

A while later, Maul walked outside to look over trees. In the last few days it had encroached all the way to the trees that surrounded his home. As far as he could see there was white death, and it was a gloomy sight. Grey clouds were gathering in the north and beyond them no sky was visible. The air was chilly and fresh. He walked around the house looking at the ash—grey limbs that reached like fingers from the spruce trees the house had been built from. He slapped a few out of his way as he circled the house and they broke off as expected and shattered to the ground.

To the rear of the house, he found that some of the branches were rubbing against the house and there were scratch marks like waves on the panelled wood there. The light was dimming with the approaching cloudbank but Maul thought he saw some white on the wall of his house and it worried him. He leaned to look better; it could just be the scratching after all; that was most likely. On closer inspection, he saw, with dismay, that he was mistaken. It was the same dead white that had been on all the trees. He wiped at it with his hands hoping it was just dust like it had been on the axe handle a week ago. To his great consternation, nothing changed at all and the wood of his home felt the same levelled smoothness as the infected trees. It made little sense and Maul didn't have time to try to make sense of it.

He ran to the shed and got a mallet and saw and came straight back to the infected site. Smashing a hole in his wall right on top of the white markings, he then used the saw to cut out a large enough area around this. He was hoping to stop the spread in the only way he knew how. Next, he took hold of one of the branches whose twig ends were burnishing the house and took the saw to it. He quickly saw that he needn't have bothered as the branch snapped like a thin sliver of ice as soon as force was applied to it. Dropping the saw he moved along the side of the house grabbing any branch or limb that he thought might possibly reach his house and tore and pulled at them until they were nothing more than brittle sheaves of chips on the ground. He did another lap of the house to both be sure no more was touching and also to see that there were no more areas where he might have to put holes in his wall.

Once this was done, Maul spent the next half hour gathering up all the wood he'd splintered with a shovel and brush and tossed them in a bucket by the front door. After this, he lit a fire in the stove and taking the bucket inside began to feed the chips and twigs in a few at a time to get rid of them for good. The brief idea came to him of setting fire to the dead trees in a bid to stop the spread of the disease outside his own land but he quickly dismissed this as ludicrous. He was not dumb enough to think he would be able to control a forest fire once he started it. The whole mountainside would go up if he tried and that would leave him in an even worse situation than now — assuming he even survived the fire.

When bedtime finally came that evening Maul was tired from all his traveling and mental anguishes of the day. He lay in bed in the pitch black and listened to the creaking forest outside. Just before bed, a light snow had started to come down, and he thought there would be a blanket of the stuff in the morning.

The dreams that visited Maul were swirling and confused and even within them he did not feel safe or at ease. Something was coming, something he didn't understand but that he knew meant him great harm and there was nothing he could do to stop it. He moved through the woods from life to white death and something followed, a heavy noise that crashed through bushes and branches and yet that he could not see. An image of the rotten wood at the mine entrance came to him and he wondered if the thing had lived there, had followed him home when it felt his evil intent. Or was it perhaps the people of the town, coming after him with pitchforks like he was some beast from a horrible fairy-tale? They hated him, he knew it and they had always wanted him, and his family before him, to leave and it looked like they meant to do it by death.

Maul sat up in panic, wild eyes staring about the room. The sweat on his body instantly turning to ice water in the cold of the night. It was silent all around and he sighed, his heart still racing. Confusion reigned a few minutes longer as he tried to figure his world out. It had been so long since he dreamed at all, let alone a bad dream, that he felt like something very unusual indeed had happened to him.

His body registered the cold in a chill shudder and he pulled the discarded blanket from the floor where it had fallen in his waking and wrapped it around his shoulders. Out the window, he could see the snow still falling, heavier now and the flakes thick and fluffy. The draft from before came over his cheeks and he looked around for the source. He didn't recall feeling this before from his bed; he'd spent a long time many years ago making his sleeping area as weather proof as possible. Then he knew where it was coming from. He'd smashed the hole in the wall earlier and had gotten into such a frenzy of lopping off limbs that he forgot to come back and patch the hole.

Maul got up and walked to the door of his room and look into the adjoining one where the hole was. A gaping hole stared back at him and some snow had drifted in and was pooling on the floor. Looking around the room, he saw nothing that would do as a plug for the night. He was still exhausted and didn't feel like going outside in the weather and getting wood from the shed to cover the gap. He looked to the room once more and lighted on the old kitchen table. It was long and oval at one end — the other end had been hacked off for some other mending job in the distant past. As it was now, he would be able to stand it on the flat end and leave it against the wall to cover the hole. Its weight would hold it in place and he could sort out the problem properly in the morning.

Maul hoisted the table up, the blanket falling from his shoulders as he did and moved it on its end to the wall. He set it down and had a look out through the hole to see how deep the snow was. It was getting deep already but something else caught his eye — around the rim of the hole, thin tendrils of twigs were scraping the wood. This wasn't possible; Maul had made sure of it before finishing up outside earlier on. The only thing he could think of was that a tree must have toppled over while he slept and was touching the house now. He pushed his head right up to the gap to see out but could see no such thing as a fallen tree. All along on either side though he saw the wavering limbs off the trees, all of them touching the house once more. A sickening feeling went through him and for one moment Maul wondered if he was still dreaming.

A sound like the lash of a whip struck the frosty air and four string like limbs shot in through the gap and grabbed Maul by the underside of the chin and base of his skull. He screamed and pressed both hands against the wall to try push himself out of the grip of whatever held him. The strength in those limbs was far too much for even Maul Thorndean, however, and he felt the pain of the branches cutting into his flesh. He pulled at the limbs, remembering how easily they had broken off when he thrashed at the once outside earlier on, but this time, the only gave a little and all the breaking power he could muster in his hands did nothing to help him. His neck distended and he heard cracking sounds in the upper spine and his neck. The warmth of blood washed over his bare chest and with one last push against the wall Maul knew that his final defeat had come.

Chapter 5

J oe Moorefield had been sheriff of Mercy for a little over five years now. He'd previously been a beat cop from small town in Ohio and had gotten the job here based on the very little experience he could speak of. His application for the job had been on a whim upon seeing a handwritten note on the bulletin board at the station. A few months passed by and then he got a call from a guy called Oakes who asked him a few questions about his work history and then offered him the job at the end of the conversation.

"There's no interview process?" Joe had asked almost laughing at the oddness.

"This was the interview process, you're the most experienced by a country mile," Oakes said.

"Where's the old sheriff going?" Joe asked wondering now was there something more sinister in this tiny town of Mercy.

"I'm retiring, heading down to Florida to get some sun for my last few years." The conversation had gone on a little longer and Joe found himself accepting the post and by Fall of that year he had upped stakes and moved to the mountains. Not that he was leaving all that much behind. His parents had passed away, and he was unmarried with no other family. The few friends he had were always wary of his being a police officer; they hadn't ever said anything to him about it but he could feel it all the same, it was like they could never be truly comfortable and themselves around him. He would be no great loss to them and he wasn't exactly shedding tears himself as he said goodbye at the small bash in Hannigan's pub they threw for him.

Five years on his number of friends had neither increased nor decreased. He was the sheriff of a town that by all rights didn't need one. The local law in Emerson should have jurisdiction over Mercy which to his mind was little more than a street, it certainly didn't deserve the moniker of 'town' to his thinking or understanding of the word. The population was about forty people over six square miles in the summer and this dropped to less than twenty during fall, winter and early spring. It baffled him how any of the businesses stayed afloat in such a place but they did.

Joe lived in the station house which had one small cell, an office and then a bedroom and kitchen cum dining room at the back. So far, the only occupant of the cell during his tenure had been Mouse Allen one night when he was too drunk to drive home and Joe too tired to drive him there. There was no life at all in the place, but Joe had to admit it was a beautiful part of the country and he enjoyed living here. He'd become something of a hiker and hunter in his time and his evenings were spent in the effort of writing a book — something else that had come to him since living in Mercy.

The snows had all but cleared over the past few days and as Joe stepped out of the station, the only evidence was the brown stained sludge piles at the side of the road. The ground was slick and wet from the melting and would remain so until some decent sun came he supposed. Jeff Sorkin was looking out the window of his store and Joe nodded in greeting to him. Jeff called some kind of greeting out but the words were lost through the glass and shut door of the store. Joe waved as if understanding and went on up the street towards the Lone Wolf.

Sally smiled at him as he came in and took out the cup and saucer for the coffee she knew he would order.

"Morning Sally," he said. "Coffee and apple pie." He ordered this every time he came into the tavern during the day, which wasn't often. Joe was very fond of Sally's pie and he had the coffee just to wash it down.

"Catch any international jewel thieves this morning Joe?" Sally asked putting his coffee down in front of him.

"Just a couple," he answered with a nod of thanks. "Had to let one go though."

"Yeah?"

"Yeah, not enough room at the jail to hold both."

"You could have locked one up in here."

"This place is too nice to be locked up in."

"I don't know about that," Sally said looking around, "I'm locked up here most of the time and I'm always aching to get out!" Joe smiled; he was very fond of Sally and wondered why she had never found herself a husband. True she would be a handful but she had a heart of gold and an easy way with everyone she ever met, even Maul Thorndean. The thought struck Joe then that he'd not seen Maul Thorndean for a long time. He knew Maul had been down only a couple of months ago but Joe had missed him that day. As he ate his pie, he thought more on this and decided that it was odd that he had not seen Maul on any of the hikes or hunts Joe had been on in that time too. Now that he was on it he didn't remember hearing Maul's old rifle booming up in the hills lately either.

"You seen Maul Thorndean of late?" he asked Sally. If anyone in town might have seen him it would be her, he supposed.

"Actually no," she said taking a serious interest. "It's funny you mention it as I would have been expecting him last week or so."

"I never noticed he came down on any schedule," Joe said wondering how he'd missed something like that.

"Well, he doesn't," Sally said, "But I generally notice when it's been a few days longer than usual and that was last week this time round."

"He might show up today then," Joe said but something in his experience told him this would not be the case.

"Maybe," Sally said but there was a look of doubt in her face for an instant and then she looked out the window to the rear of the galley kitchen. Joe wondered what she was thinking but decided to let it rest for now.

The day passed much as ever when Joe left the tavern. People from town would engage him in conversation and let him know the same pet peeves they had with their neighbours — mostly those who didn't live here in winter but would be back in only a matter of weeks now for the end of the spring season and summer. Joe would listen politely to their inane gripes and tell them once again that what the neighbours did was not against the law and he could do nothing about it unless it crossed that line. The stock response to this was always a look of disgust and a shake of the head,

"Well it should be against the law!"

All of this jawing and then helping Jeff Sorkin move some lumber to get to his water tank that was not heating properly took his focus from Maul Thorndean and his intention of going up to check on the old man. Joe wasn't worried exactly; he thought it would take quite a bit to knock that old buzzard of his perch, but he would be remiss if he didn't check on Maul occasionally just to be sure he was doing alright.

By the time the idea of going up there came again, it was growing dark and to his dismay the snow piled down again as heavy as it had the last few weeks before. The trip up mountain would have to wait until light. As the end of his official working hours came — there was no such thing really — he stepped out of his little office and looked at the street covered in snow. Voices came to him from a little away and he looked up to see Mouse Allen and Jeff going into the tavern. The desire for a beer came over Joe. Why not, he thought, he could ask anyone who was in there too if they had seen Maul. Killing two birds with one stone, wasn't that what they called it. He was sure one of the others would have seen Maul on their travels over the hills.

The heat inside the tavern hit Joe as soon as he entered from the street. All eyes in the place looked to him when he came in and silence fell over the conversation — nothing new there at least.

"Come in for the heat, Joe?" Jeff asked.

"That and a beer," Joe said nodding to Sally who pulled one for him. "And I was wondering if anyone has seen Maul Thorndean lately?" he added. At this, everyone looked around at one another in surprise.

"Why are you looking for him?" Mouse asked, his eyebrows raised.

"I want to make sure he's alright, I haven't seen him in weeks now, so I'm hoping someone here has to ease my mind on his safety."

"Well," Mouse said, losing interest now that Maul was not a wanted man. "The last time I saw him was when he was here about six or seven weeks ago."

"Same for me," Jeff nodded agreement.

"Anyone else seen him since?" Joe asked looking around the room, "Even a glimpse?" he added when no one answered him.

"I saw him a good few weeks ago, after he was in town," Sam Brainard said from his table. Now all eyes on the room were on him. Joe walked over closer and looked at him,

"Where, Sam?"

"I was chopping a mile or so from his land," Sam said, "when he came up with a lump of wood in his hands."

"What wood?"

"Part of a trunk from his land; he was worried about some disease his trees had and he asked me to come and look."

"Why did he ask you to do that?" Joe asked.

"I don't know really, I guess he thought since I worked with trees I might know something about it," Sam said with a shrug of his shoulders.

"And did you?" Joe asked. Sam shook his head, looking a little embarrassed by this,

"No, I hadn't seen anything like it before," he said.

"You went up to his land?" Mouse asked incredulous. "I'm surprised you're still counted among the living."

"I didn't go to his land, the disease had spread beyond and he showed me some trees that had it," Sam said defensively. Joe wanted to ask more about the disease but he thought he should focus on Maul.

"What happened then?" he asked.

"Nothing, I said I'd look it up in one of my books and get back to him if I could find anything out."

"Did you find what it was?" This voice was Sally Briers from behind the bar. Sam looked over to her,

"No, nothing I could find sounded like what's out there."

"So you left Maul, and that was the last you saw of him?" Joe asked. Sam nodded, "How did he seem?" Joe asked.

"About the same as I ever saw him," Sam said noncommittally.

"Crazy as fuck you mean!" Mouse cackled and a few people laughed along with him.

"He didn't seem sick or ill or anything to you?" Joe asked ignoring this. Again, Sam shook his head but Joe was unsure, he felt there was something Sam was not telling him and he meant to find out when there wasn't so much of an audience.

"Thanks, Sam," he said taking his drink from the bar. "Now, if no one else has seen him since then I'll go off duty at this point!"

There was no answer and Joe took a swig of his beer and sat down at a table close to the bar. As Joe expected, a conversation started up with people recalling things that had happened involving the Thorndean family over the many years. There was not one person in the room who could attest to first-hand knowledge of any of the old stories they told but there was also not one of them who had any doubt about their veracity. Joe would go up there in the morning and see what was going on with the old man. He was probably fine and would curse Joe to hell for coming near his land, but if that was the worst of it, that would be a good outcome. Something inside told him this would not be the case, he didn't know what it was or why he felt this way, but it was there. He didn't think there was a good ending to this one.

Chapter 6

The old Buick spurted a plume of dark smoke that diffused in the air in the starkest of contrasts to the gleaming white of snow gathering on the road.

"It's getting worse, Jarrod," the female passenger said looking out through the back window. She was getting frightened now that the dark had closed in around them and the car was failing.

"Don't worry, Ava," the driver said, "this old car hasn't let me down yet!" The smile he flashed her was one of complete confidence in what he was saying and she smiled back too. He reached out and took her hand, squeezing it tenderly.

"I still think we should have stopped in that last town," Ava said.

"They said there's another town just up the road, here," Jarrod said nodding to the black road ahead. Ava looked there too but could see very little and certainly nothing that could be mistaken for the lights of a town on up ahead. Trust him, she told herself, he is your husband now. The term 'better or worse' rang out in her memory and she smiled. "That's my girl!" Jarrod said when he saw her smile and this only broadened it, lighting up her entire face.

Jarrod, for his part, was far too excited with life right then and all he could think about was getting to California as fast as they could. If someone could invent the car that could drive itself he would happily sleep on the road. He was still in shock that not only had Ava married him against her family's wishes but that she had also committed to going west with him. For the first time in his life, he felt free, and it was as if something infused within his soul. All he could see in his mind was the sun of California and Ava and him going about their days in blissful happiness.

The car spluttered again and backfired more of that black smoke and this time he wasn't so sure all was rosy underneath the hood after all, perhaps it would be best to get to this next town sooner rather than later. He didn't like the idea of getting stranded on a cold mountainside with next to nothing to eat and only their extra clothes to keep them warm. He chanced pressing down on the gas a little more; the people in Emerson had said Mercy was only ten miles away after all. They should almost be there by now if the odometer was anything to go by.

Jarrod's prayers — and Ava's too — were answered when they crested a rise in the road and saw the houses in the road ahead.

"What did I tell you," he said leaning his head towards Ava.

"Is this it?" Ava said still looking ahead. "There doesn't seem to be much to it."

"They said it was small, but there was a tavern we could stay at."

"That must be it over there," Ava said pointing to the only building that even had a light on.

Jarrod was aware then someone was looking at him and he saw a man standing in a doorway looking out at them curiously. Jarrod waved but continued on to the lights of the tavern and pulled up.

"Wait here and I'll make sure there's a room for us," Jarrod said. Ava nodded, and he jumped out of the car and went inside.

While he was gone, Ava checked in her purse once again for their marriage license. They were both young, and she was sure they would have to produce it everywhere they went on their way to the coast. Looking out through the windows of the car, she felt the darkness of the night all around her. She worried now about getting a room. If they didn't get one here, they would have to go all the way back to Emerson to stay, and she didn't like the idea of that last drive either. Jarrod's face when he came back out told her she need worry no more on that score.

"Come on," he said pulling her door open. "There's a couple of steaks on for us and the landlady said she'd set up a bed for us while we eat." His smile was infectious and the idea of the food and the warm bed filled her with joy. She leaped out, and he took her in his arms and spun around laughing before going inside out of the snow.

The tavern was very warm and a low fire sparked in the grate on the wall to the right as they came in. There were plenty of free tables and she saw the one she wanted right off. Some customers looked them up and down and nodded hello as Jarrod guided her to the bar.

"This is my wife Ava," he said to a large, though by no means fat, woman behind the counter.

"Sally's my name," she said with a smile. "Your steaks are on, so why don't you take up a seat and warm up over there."

"Thank you very much," Ava said, "You have a lovely place here."

"Shame about the clientele, though," Sally said and laughed. No one else laughed and Ava was suddenly very embarrassed and not sure at all how to react to this. "Don't mind them, they're all sour about the snow starting up again," Sally said to her and then Jarrod led her over to the very table she had thought would be best.

Soon after steak and vegetables were placed in front of them both and Sally announced that she was going up to make up a room and no one would get another drink for at least ten minutes. While she was away, the other customers talked lowly amongst themselves and looked at them now and then.

"You come in from Emerson?" an older man asked when Jarrod met eyes with him.

"We did," he answered with a friendly smile.

"How come you didn't stay there overnight?" a big man sitting with the older man asked.

"We're heading to California and every mile we can get done in a day counts," Jarrod said. The man looked at him for a few moments with a very serious look on his face,

"You're lucky to make it here at all in the dark," he said.

"Oh. The road wasn't so bad."

"I wasn't talking about the road," the man said and he looked around the room in a way that made both Jarrod and Ava wonder what it was he was not telling them. They exchanged a nervous glance.

"Then what are you talking about?" Ava asked, her voice barely more than a cracked a whisper. Her hand reached out and took hold of Jarrod's. The man at the bar looked at his neighbour and then around the bar before looking back to the couple and leaning forward in his seat like he would whisper some dark secret to them.

"We don't know ourselves," he said conspiratorially, "but there's something out there in those woods that surround us."

"What, an animal of some sort?" Jarrod laughed, but the laugh was nervous.

"Like I say," the man said. "We don't know what it is. It could be an animal but it doesn't leave the tracks of anyone I know about, or want to!"

"You got that right, Mouse," the man beside him chimed in. Ava looked to Jarrod to see his reaction to this, but she saw that his own eyes were darting around the room to gauge the other people there. That was all she needed to see to know that Jarrod didn't know whether or not to believe this story.

"What's it done?" Jarrod asked after his scan.

"Killed livestock mostly," Mouse said.

"What kind?"

"Everything from chicken to cow," Mouse said and then turning to the man next to him said, "You lost a dog too, wasn't it Jeff?"

"That's right," Jeff said nodding glumly. Now Ava really was scared and wished they had stayed in Emerson. She had never liked the woods even in daylight and now it was pitch black for who knew how many miles around them.

"What was your dog's name?" Jarrod asked with a sly smile on his face.

"Toby," Jeff answered without a beat. This seemed to surprise Jarrod who Ava felt must have doubted the story to ask in the first place.

"Leave it off, guys," a younger man said from the table by the fireside. His corner was darker and out of the direct heat of the fire but his eyes looked to the strangers and they were kind. Mouse and Jeff also looked over at the man.

"You think we should let these people walk around Mercy without telling them of the monster that lives up the hill, Sam?" Mouse asked. Sam shook his head and looked back to the couple as he answered this,

"I think we should let these people have their dinner and get a good night's sleep without having nightmares about a man you don't like."

"A man?" Mouse said almost indignant "The name beast is too good for him, even creature is too kind!" Ava didn't like the sound of whoever this man was talking about but she was very at least that it was a man and not some fairy-tale wolf or demon of the forest.

"I'm not having this same conversation again," Sam said. "We had it earlier when the sheriff was here and there's no need to go over it again."

"Over what again?" Sally said coming back into the room.

"Nothing," Mouse said turning back to the bar like a slinking schoolboy caught at some mischief

"Maul Thorndean?" Sally asked, and she looked to Sam to answer. He nodded and Sally shook her head. She looked to the couple.

"I hope these idiots haven't been trying to scare you with their rubbish?" she said apologetically

"Not at all," Jarrod said in better humour now. "They were just razzing us." His smile was bright and cheery and Ava couldn't help but mirror it in her relief. She would be happy to get to bed away from these people all the same.

Later that night, when they were alone in their room, Jarrod could see that Ava was still apprehensive about being there. They had changed into their bedclothes and Ava was sitting on the side of the bed using her reflection in the window to comb her hair. He looked at her for a moment and smiled — that was all he seemed to do nowadays, ever since he first met her.

"Don't worry," he said sitting down behind her and putting a hand on her back. "We'll be gone straight after breakfast." The idea of what that woman Sally might serve up in the morning filled him with salivating desire, despite his belly still being full from the dinner they'd recently eaten. Ava leaned back into his hand and paused in her brushing a moment to regard him in the reflection.

"How long until we can see the ocean, do you think?" she asked.

"Another few days," he answered. "Has to be getting close now after all this driving." Ava nodded satisfied with this answer and went back to her hair. Jarrod rubbed her back once more and then lay back on the bed with his hands over his belly. He couldn't imagine being more contented that he was at that moment. Soon, while Ava still silently brushed away, he started to drift off to sleep.

The scream that shook him from the pleasant slumber was the most shocking thing he'd ever heard in his life. He sat bolt up, seeing Ava but not knowing where they were.

"What? What is it!" he asked standing up and looking around the strange room.

"Someone was out there!" Ava said taking hold of his arm and pulling her body close to his. She was white and trembling and tears were gathering in her eyes.

"What? Who?" Jarrod asked as he finally came to know where he was and what was happening — or at least what Ava thought was happening. The lamp was off now but the light of the moon was bright enough that he was getting a clearer look at his surroundings. He looked through the glass to the outside going no closer to it and then put his arm around Ava and guided back to a sitting position on the bed

"When I turned out the light I saw a face," Ava said and now the tears came. "It wasn't like any face I've ever seen!" Her head collapsed into his chest as her torso heaved with sobbing.

"Don't worry, darling, it's alright," Jarrod said and he rubbed her hair and rocked her back and forth like a child.

"Did you see it?" she asked looking up into his face to see his reaction.

"I didn't see anything," he said and then with a sigh, "I don't think you did either, Ava. I think what those men downstairs were saying got into your head and has been playing on your mind."

"This was real!" she said pushing away from him suddenly as though he was scorching hot.

"Ava!" he pleaded.

"No," she shouted. "I know what I saw, it wasn't a nightmare; I wasn't the one snoring asleep on the bed I'm wide awake!"

"Alright," Jarrod said in a soothing calm voice, "I'll go take a look."

He walked to the window and looked up and down outside; there was a clear area for a few yards and then the treeline started and it was a very short distance into that he could see despite the bright moon and the thick snow blanketed everywhere. He made a show of looking for a long time as he didn't believe she had seen anything and even if she had it was most likely one of the local men trying to get a look at Ava in her nightclothes — not something he liked the idea but nothing that worried him a whole lot or made him nervous.

"Anything?" Ava asked, a lilt of hope in her voice.

"Nothing," he said, "and I don't see any footprints in the snow either." He turned and looked at her and this final point seemed to be what convinced her Jarrod may have been right after all. Perhaps the story of the man up the hill had scared her so much that when she plunged herself into darkness, she was still seeing her own reflection in the glass and got spooked by it.

"I'm sorry," she said, "Let's just go to sleep." She got into the bed as he watched her.

"You think you're going to be able to sleep now?" he asked. She nodded vigorously and lay down as if this proved it.

"Alright," Jarrod said getting in beside her and taking her into his arms.

Outside the snow trickled down some more. The ground beneath the window and leading to the woods bore no footprints at all.

Chapter 7

S am Brainard wiped the sweat from his brow and fought back another wave of nausea. His sleeve felt rough on his forehead and the sound was like some factory machine in his head. He looked around at the paltry amount of logs around him and looked up into the sky inhaling deeply as annoyance came into him.

He'd not intended last night's drinking to be any worse than most nights he spent in the tavern, but he had one more than usual when he was tempted on his way out and that led to a return round and then Sally was spreading some out for free as she did from time to time. The result was the mashing hangover that now saw in his hollow skull, pounding and banging louder than any axe blow Sam had ever laid against a tree. He wished he could vomit but not being able to face a breakfast this morning all but ruled that out. Lifting the axe, he struck again and once more he was almost out of breath with the effort. This was unbelievable — he was a young man in the prime of life who could chop and log trees all day under normal circumstances

"Fuck!" he shouted into the crisp air and even this had much less power than he'd hoped; the snow all around him dampening the sound of his anger. He spat the tangy saliva from his mouth and watched it dissolve into the blanket by his feet. It would not be a productive day, but he felt he should go on trying all the same. Perhaps he'd feel better in a while and the pace would pick up, he thought. The sweat was back at his brow and though he knew it was not a wise thing to do, he took off his fleece-lined jacket to continue his work.

The breath of the cold on his body as it seeped through the fibres of his shirt and vest was at once calming and rejuvenating. It was so pleasant that he let his axe down a moment and went to sit on the wide stump of an old elm tree that had been cut down before they were wiped out in the area. Leaning with his elbows on his knees, he looked around again at the snowy wilderness around him and it made him feel better. Despite the extra hardships the snow brought, there was no denying its beauty. Just like there was no denying the beauty of Susan Bloom, he thought. Her creamy skinned face rose up in his mind and the goofy smile that came with it made him giddy and he chuckled at his childish foolishness.

Sam had liked Susan since the day he came to Mercy, but so far she had shown no interest in him. She was always pleasant and would stop and chat if he engaged her, leaving him feeling on top of the world each time, but never giving him even the hint of reciprocal interest.

"That doesn't mean anything, though," he said aloud. "Women are strange creatures." He nodded in agreement with his own statement and rose up back to his work.

As he cut, more slowly than before, he thought more about Susan and he determined that he would ask her out that very day, as soon as he got back to town. Another flush of giddiness coursed through him and he shook his head smiling. How weak he was to control himself when it came to thoughts of her. If only she would say yes that would make things here a whole lot better. A couple more swings of the axe knocked the breath out of him again, and with it the courage to talk to Susan today. He was in no state to be asking anything of her with this hangover. Susan would be apt to run a mile from the smell of the beer that emanated from his skin.

A noise from back down towards the road stopped him from dwelling on this thought. Sam peered through the trees in an effort to see what it was. As he did the sound of a revved engine in gear change floated up to him. It was hard to make out, but he thought it was sheriff Moorefield's jeep. He was heading up the hill and Sam wondered where he was going. Then he recalled Joe had been looking about Maul Thorndean and it was most likely that he was going up there to check on the hermit.

"Better you, than me, Joe," Sam said looking after the car the sound receded.

Sam's thoughts went back to the day Maul had come to him with the diseased wood and then knocked him down the hill. His back had been covered in bruises for a few days after that. He had told no one in town what had happened but he didn't know if that was to stop more stories about Maul spreading or because he was embarrassed that he had been so frightened of the old man. He would like to think it was the former, but he felt it was more likely the latter. Though as he thought about it, what did he have to be embarrassed about in that regard? Mouse Allen was fond of talking himself up and was a huge fella and though he talked big when Maul came to town, it was clear to everyone that even he was afraid of the wild man from the top of the mountain. Maybe Maul was like something from a fairy tale, he thought recalling Mouse and Jeff trying to scare that couple who came into the tavern last night. The only people who didn't seem afraid of him were Joe and Sally, and Sam didn't know if they were right not to be worried by him.

The sound of the jeep finally stopped and the briefest moment of silence was punctuated by a creak of wood somewhere nearby. Sam looked around in surprise at the sound but saw nothing. It had sounded like something heavy leaning against one of the younger trunks and that meant it was something of large size. His immediate thought was a wolf watching him from some as yet unrevealed hiding place. Sam could feel eyes on him and he was very suddenly completely unnerved. Clutching the axe he got himself on a firmer footing and looked around, not moving nor making a sound. He stood there like that for the better part of a minute but still nothing else disturbed the silence.

His heart beat heavily in his chest as he eased up. It was unlikely to be a wolf at this time of day and there was not much to hide behind in this cleared area. If something had been here, he was sure he would have seen some trace of it in that time he'd scanned the ground surrounding him.

"This bloody hangover has me all over the place," he said, his own voice a reassuring noise against the thick silence. He looked around again and then thought it odd that no birds had been making any noise anywhere in the forest. He listened out but there was nothing and he looked up into the branches as far as he could see and saw no evidence of any feathered beasts at all. This was unusual, he thought. That it might have something to do with the disease Maul had shown him came to Sam at the very same instant that he saw a cluster of trees whose bark looked white and bleached. He looked around once more and then walked over to it. Feeling the bark, he saw that it was the same as the wood Maul had brought to him. Remembering how weak that had been Sam half raised his axe and let it fall against the bark. To his shock and surprise, the young tree snapped in two with a loud crack and fell. He jumped back though it fell away from him and looked in wonder as it took down two more trees in its fall.

"Well, I'll be damned," Sam said looking at the site of the felled trees. "If only they were all that easy!"

Like the prick of a needle on the back of his neck, Sam suddenly felt like there were malevolent eyes on him once more. The surrounding silence made the feeling even more pervasive, and he shot nervous searching glances about in all directions.

"Who's there?" he called out and he could hear the nerves in the timbre of his voice and he inwardly cursed knowing that whoever was watching him would know that he was scared. "Maul?" he asked then, knowing that it could only be him. Who else would sneak around in the woods this far from town and not show themselves? It was Maul, he was more sure of it by the second but it didn't ease his mind to think it. Sam had seen the dark side of Maul in that flash of anger before and he didn't want to see any more of it. Maul probably considered Sam an enemy now, especially since Sam had not come back to help with the disease in the trees. The thought of this made him look back at the felled trees once more. What the hell was this, and how far was it going to spread? Was it possible the whole forest could soon be wiped out?

Sam walked back to his pack and took it up, looking around him all the while as he did. He felt afraid and paranoid and he wanted to be out of this place. He consoled himself that it was all part of the hangover and then he could come back tomorrow and get back to work as normal. All he needed was a decent night's sleep.

As he walked back towards the road where his car awaited him, he could hear creaking and cracking in the woods behind him. It was as though someone was following him and close by, but each time he turned to look he could see nothing and as he got closer to the road, there was less and less for anyone to hide behind. The sounds followed him all the way and even when he was in his car he could still hear it as though it were right beside his open window. It was freaky, and he was scared of it. The sweat on his forehead was greasy with the alcohol emission and he felt nauseous again. All he wanted to do was to get out of here. Taking off the handbrake, he let the car roll down the hill on its own before turning the key in the ignition.

It felt good to be going away, but he was all the way back into town before he felt the eyes lift from him.

"Has to be the hangover," he said as he parked outside his home. Sam went inside and straight to his bedroom and lay down. He had never been delirious with drink before but he had a feeling he had just had his first experience of it up the mountain. He just hoped he would be able to sleep well so he could laugh it off in the morning.

The last thing he saw in his mind's eye was a pair of inhuman eyes peering out at him from the darkness of the trees. He knew that it would not be a pleasant sleep but he would have to get through it. Outside the quiet town went on as ever, a car passing by every now and then or the sound of footsteps on the road crunching through the new snow. Sam closed his eyes and sighed into darkness

Chapter 8

Even standing outside the sheriff's office, Joe felt apprehensive about the day ahead. Either way things were not going to go well for him this morning. If, as he feared, something had happened to Maul Thorndean, Joe would be the man to find him and have to deal with it. On the other hand, if Maul was fine there were going to be harsh words coming from him on seeing the law on his land — and with a temperament like Maul's there was no telling where that might end up.

The snow had come down steadily all night and there was a covering all around, even the dirty sludge at the sides of the road had been given a new powdered layer making the whole place look a lot prettier than it had been yesterday. No living thing showed on the street and all was quiet. It would be a perfect morning for a short hike up around the old mine shafts but that was not his destiny today. Perhaps tomorrow, if today goes well, he thought.

Joe checked over his gun and gear one last time, gave the jeep a look over and then set off up the road. He drove slowly, getting a feel for the icy road and looking out left and right into the trees as he went. You never knew when Maul would show up in town and it was as likely Joe could pass him on the way as not. The only thing Joe saw on the way up to the Thorndean place was Sam Brainard's car parked at the side of the road. It was generally close to this spot when Joe passed here. Sam was clearing a space to build himself a home and had been at it for a long time; no doubt he had plans to marry and hoped this would be something to offer a prospective bride.

Joe had picked up speed at this point thinking it better to get to where he was going quickly and get it done with. The snow on the road seemed to be thicker further up, and the jeep felt a little unwieldy especially on the banked curves.

"This could get a little tricky," he said and hoped that he would not have to walk any of the way.

About a half-mile from the Thorndean place the gradient steepened and the wheels slipped more often. Joe dropped to a lower gear to combat this and tried to straddle the centre of the road to make use of the slant on either side from that point. Each time the car slid, he thought it would be best to stop and walk, but he persevered, praising and talking softly to the automobile like it was a frightened horse crossing deep water. It was a relief to pull up on the dirt path that led into the woods where Maul Thorndean's house lay shrouded.

As Joe got out of the car and stood there, he was struck at once by the abject silence of the place. There was no noise at all save the hot exhaust of his jeep ticking over as it died down after use. He looked around and was taken aback by just how white everything was here, it looked like the snow had even stuck to the bark of the trees but he knew that couldn't be the case and assumed it was some kind of reflection that didn't happen for whatever reason lower down the mountainside.

The beat up ground was hard and crunched under his feet as he walked up what was once the drive to the house. There were two rotted wooden poles that had once held up the gates of the family home. Joe wondered how long ago since any gate was here at all. There was a worn path through the ground but all around was overgrown — or at least would be in summer, now it was all bare twigged bushes and some ground level vegetation. Looking down he saw that the bushes had the same white on them too and he saw now that it was not a reflection — the wood looked old and scarred by fire. He bent down and snapped off a twig and it came off so easily in his hand he barely had to make an effort at all.

This was odd, but not odd enough to stop him here. Joe walked on along the track and soon saw that all of the trees here had the same white bark like there had been a huge fire but there were no scorch marks anywhere, only this whiteness.

"What in the hell is this?" he said looking around. There had certainly been no fire; the scale of it would have been visible for miles around if all these trees had gone up. Joe realised that he had stopped walking and forced himself to go on. He couldn't take his eyes from the devastation around him and then as he got closer to the house he saw that all of the trees were leaning in the same way he was going like they had been set to point him to the house. They got lower and lower until they were parallel to ground at only the height of Joe's chest.

Now he was able to see the house, and he gasped at the sight. The trees in a circle all around leaned to the house at the centre and the wood of the house was the exact same as the bark of the trees. It made no sense to Joe at all. He stopped walking again, but this time it was because he was nervous. This was a new situation for him, a situation he had never even heard about or considered before. His first thought was that Maul had done this but that didn't seem possible. But then, if Maul hadn't done this, what in the hell had? Joe looked to the house for some movement but it was hard to see in with all the low trees.

"Maul?" he called out. No answer. "Maul!" he called again, louder this time. Still only silence. And yet, Joe felt the man was here, or someone was. "Maul, I'm coming into the house to see if you are alright!" If anything would set Maul off it would be the idea of the police coming into his home. But still, there was nothing, not a sound. Joe pulled his gun and looked around again, he felt someone here. Back in the city, he would have radioed for back up, but he never thought such a thing would ever happen here in sleepy Mercy. The urge to leave came for a moment but he knew he couldn't; he would have to go into the house and see if there was anyone in there.

Gripping his gun in front of him, Joe made his way to the house, having to climb over or go under some limbs that blocked his way. He could see the footprints on the ground beneath him that showed that until recently this area had been clear and Maul had been able to walk through as normal. This only raised more questions that Joe didn't have time to think about right now. He called again when he was a few feet from the house but was once more greeted only with silence. The very depth of the silence was unnerving, like it was purposeful somehow.

The front door was ajar and Joe peered in seeing the cold stove with no sign of recent heat from it. He'd never been this close to the house before so would have no idea if things seemed out of place. A single chair stood in the centre of the room but that was all. Joe had always imagined — though this was the first time he consciously knew this — that Maul's place would be kitted out in furniture made from wood from the forest and decorated with animal hides and elk heads from hunting. As he looked in further, he saw that it was practically barren and a twinge of sorrow for Maul's life affected him for a moment.

Something odd then caught his eye. There was a table, large enough to seat six people comfortably, propped up against the back wall of the room. The legs jutted out towards the door as Joe stepped inside. Just to the right of this there was a large hole in the wall where snow had come in and gathered on the floor inside

"What caused that?" he wondered aloud. Stepping inside he saw a rifle leaning against the wall at the door. He leaned down and picked it up. On seeing it was loaded he opened the barrel and took out the rounds inside before placing the gun back on the ground.

Joe went through the few rooms of the house slowly, listening carefully outside each room before he went inside. There was no sign of anything and some of the rooms probably hadn't seen life in many years. Dust and cobwebs covered what little was there, and no footprints disturbed the covering on the floor.

When he was sure the house was empty, he went back down to the first room and looked again at the hole. It was a strange place for there to be a hole, especially when there was nothing around the room that might have made it — unless it was one of the legs of the table. Or perhaps it was a gunshot, but it didn't look like one. Joe leaned to the wood and saw that the edges were facing inwards — which meant the hole was made from the outside. All Joe could see through the hole was the trees that lay against the house and he didn't see how anything could've gotten close enough to do this kind of damage from out there.

Joe felt uneasy here but there had been no sign so far that anything might have happened to Maul. His gun was here, that was perhaps a little odd, but surely he could carry his gun all the time up here? He felt some wood shards under his feet and he crouched down to sift the snow and look at it. It was splinters from the shattered wall and there was no large part at all but only all small pieces of debris. It led him to think that it must have been some blow that did the damage to break the wood up like this.

Something small caught his eye then and Joe looked carefully before touching near it. Some of the snow he'd disturbed had clumped together in tiny red smudges and Joe thought it was possibly blood. There wasn't enough of it to make it any kind of a crime scene — Maul had probably cut himself trying to free up a bit of the wall that was flapping loose — but it was enough to raise the sheriff's suspicions and add to his feeling of unease.

Joe spent another half hour at the house and then did his best to look around the land for another hour after that but came up with nothing at all. It was as if Maul Thorndean had simply vanished off the earth.

Chapter 9

Susan Bloom looked after the sheriff as he walked away from her. She had been coming home from the store when she met him and he asked if she had seen Maul Thorndean lately. The very utterance of the man's name was enough to make her feel hostile, and she told Joe she'd not seen him for many months and would not be sorry if she never saw him again. Joe didn't act surprised at this and Susan assumed that someone had filled him in on the fight between her own father and Maul long ago.

Susan had only been a teenager when it happened but she still recalled it vividly. It had only been a month since her mother had passed away and her father had been hitting the bottle a little heavy. She could not to this day blame him for that, it was his way of coping and Susan could respect that. Clarence Bloom was not the talking kind, and this was his way. Unfortunately, it was this drinking that had led him to yell at Maul as he came through town one day.

"Why don't you and the rest of your family curl up and die!" Clarence said as Maul passed the house on his way into town only a few yards further on. Susan had heard him say this from inside and she came out wondering who on earth he could have been talking to like that. She grew terrified when she saw Maul standing there looking at her father with a perplexed look on his face. She knew his reputation for wildness, even unprovoked she'd heard, but she also knew that he lived alone up the mountain and that had no family left at all.

"He's confusing you with someone else," she said nervously trying to smile and take hold of her father's arm at the same time. "Obviously, as you don't have family up there," she added hoping this would convince. Maul stood there saying nothing, he glanced at her once and then looked back at Clarence.

"I know who I'm talking about!" he said pulling his arm free and stepping down into the street in front of Maul. "You fuckin' Thorndean's are all the same!"

"Dad..." Susan never finished trying to stop him. At what seemed the same moment, Maul's bag hit the ground and his fist slammed hard as brick into her father's face. Clarence fell back and tripped on his step, his hand went to his face and Susan could see blood pouring out through his fingers.

"Oh God, Daddy!" she called out and ran to him. He pushed her hands away and sat up spitting a huge gob of bloody phlegm to the ground and then looked up at Maul who was standing there like nothing had happened.

"I'll make you regret that," Clarence said pointing at Maul, but he did not try to get up.

Susan had wondered for a long time afterwards why he'd stayed down and it was years later when she understood that he knew he wouldn't be able to get back up, his legs were probably like jelly. Maul had walked back towards his home, not bothering to go into town now after this and without uttering a word. She had hated him from that day on and had never let him pass without scowling at him — not that it seemed to make any difference to him. Clarence never did get his revenge on Maul and he died himself two years ago now, a peaceful death in his sleep and one Susan was sure he would have wanted.

Looking after the sheriff Susan found that she was annoyed at him for making her think of that animal. Why did he care if Maul was missing, it wouldn't make any difference to anyone else's life and Maul was no lover of the law either — Joe was as likely as anyone else to fall foul of one his attacks.

Susan turned her back to the town and walked for home. In her annoyance, she wasn't careful of her footing and she slipped on the icy layer atop some of the packed snow. She managed to stay up by planting her feet and flailing her arms a moment but it was at the cost of her groceries which spiralled out of the now torn paper bag and clattered to the road.

"Damn!" she said looking over the goods hoping that nothing was damaged or leaking. The voice came just as she was bending down to pick her things up.

"Let me help you with that," it said. Susan looked to the crunching footsteps and saw it was Sam Brainard. He skidded a little on the ice as he came to a stop and almost fell over too.

"You won't be much help flat on your back," she smiled. Sam's face flashed crimson and in that moment Susan knew he was attracted to her and it came as something of a shock to her. It was so surprising that she felt her own face grow warm.

"You didn't hurt yourself, did you?" he asked as he hunkered down and gathered up her things.

"No, thankfully," she said joining him in the collecting. She was about to say 'nothing hurt but my pride,' but it felt silly and she held her tongue.

"The sheriff still looking for Maul?" Sam asked nodding back towards the way Joe had gone. Susan knew then that Sam must have been watching them as they spoke and probably saw her getting angry.

"Yes," she answered not sure if she should let Sam know too how she felt about Maul. "He'll turn up," she said then. "Who knows where he is most of the time, anyway?"

"I guess so," Sam agreed, "I see him from time to time in the woods but always at a distance."

"How's the clearing looking?" she asked happy to change the subject

"It's looking good; I hope to start building in a few weeks."

"Oh, really? How far from town is it?"

"Only about a mile," Sam said, looking happy that she was showing an interest. He stood up now with most of her groceries in his arms.

"The bag's busted," Susan said apologetically holding it out.

"No problem, I'll carry it to your house, it's only a few feet away after all."

"Thanks." There was nothing else she could have said really, save taking everything into her own arms and struggling home. In saying yes, however, it suddenly felt somehow like a date and she grew a little nervous around him.

They walked in silence for a moment and she wished he would say something more — they were going to be at her door in only a minute. She had been so taken by surprise by his feelings and even more so by her own that she didn't know what to say at all.

"I could probably do with a woman's eye on the design of the house before I start building," he said. "Maybe you'd take a look for me and tell me what you think?"

"Are you asking me out on a date?" Susan said shocked at her own playfulness. Deeper red infused Sam's face, and he looked at the ground.

"Well, I guess you could call it that," he said in a way that was supposed to be as playful but didn't come across at all the way he wanted. Susan laughed.

"Well, I guess it's a date then!" Sam looked up at her in surprise but smiled at the same time.

"Tonight?" he asked. Susan looked at him a moment and thought he looked tired.

"How about tomorrow night?" she suggested. He nodded.

"Tomorrow it is."

They started walking again and got to the steps up to her door.

"Just dump those things on the board there, and thanks for the help," Susan said.

"Think nothing of it," he said letting the goods down gently onto the stoop.

"See you tomorrow night at eight?" she said, and he nodded.

"Eight sounds great," he said.

Chapter 10

Joe had been so mystified by what he'd seen up at the Thorndean place, that on his way back to his office he only stopped to ask Susan Bloom when she had last seen Maul. There was some family history there, which Joe knew about but couldn't recall the exact details, and she didn't seem to want to help. Even if she had seen Maul she certainly wasn't saying. Joe had asked everyone else in town so he secluded himself in the office for the rest of the day catching up on paperwork that had accumulated over the last few months.

"Why do you do this?" he asked in exasperation. If he did the paperwork as it arose it would only take seconds each day but he always let it build up for months and then grew frustrated with the pile of papers that confronted him when he finally sat down to do it. He grumbled on but got it all done; promising himself that he wouldn't let it accumulate like this again.

The sheriff didn't leave his home for the rest of that day. He wouldn't be long thinking about something before the sight back up the mountain invaded his thoughts again. It was astounding, really, like nothing he'd ever even heard of. Each time he thought of it he kept ending up back at the same question: how long ago had this happened? He told himself over and again that it couldn't be recent and yet he thought he'd been up that way not too long ago — he couldn't recall when exactly, but surely not long enough for a huge chunk of the forest to have died and dried out.

His constant mental jarring tired him and he went to bed that evening earlier than would be usual for him. He had determined that Maul must have moved out of that house some time ago and the new question he would bring to the townspeople would be, do you know where Maul Thorndean is living now?

Joe's night was plagued with bad dreams; not so bad as to be called nightmares, but bad in the sense that he would awaken from each one feeling very strange and wondering for a moment where he was and if, in fact, he was still alone. More than once, he got up and looked around the house checking doors and windows before going back to bed. As a result of all this when morning came he did not feel rested at all.

Setting out into the cold, he saw that the snow had deepened considerably overnight, and he had a hazy recollection of seeing it coming down heavily during the night. The road was as quiet as ever and he set off up the hill to see who was about.

The store was open and Joe went in and found it empty.

"Jeff?" he called out.

"That you, sheriff?" came the reply.

"Yeah," Joe said glancing over some of the goods as he waited for Jeff to appear.

"What can I do for you, sheriff?" Jeff said coming from the back and extending a hand for Joe to shake. Joe smiled and shook thinking how different this man was when you were in his store when he wanted your money.

"I'm not here to buy at the minute," Joe said and he could see the drop in the storekeeper's smile though he did a decent job of hiding it. "I was up at the Thorndean place yesterday and it looks like the place has been abandoned for a long time."

"Really?" Jeff said and there was no mistaking the earnestness of his surprise.

"Sure looks that way," Joe nodded.

"You think he's gone?" A look of hope dazzled Jeff's face as he asked this and then seeing Joe's reaction to this he backtracked. "I don't mean dead, sheriff," he laughed nervously, "I meant left the mountain?

"I don't think he's gone; he's been in town since I guess his place was vacated. I suppose he'd been living somewhere else but I don't know where that might be." Jeff nodded at this with a look of concentration on his face.

"I don't know where that could be, apart from his own place there's no other building on the mountain outside Mercy that I know of."

"I'm hoping someone does know of such a place," Joe said seeing that his visit here was wasted.

"Mouse or that young fella, Sam, would probably be your best bet, although I don't know if either of them has seen any more of the forest than you have on your hikes since you got here."

"Well, maybe they have, I'm sure there's a lot I still haven't seen."

When he left the store, he crossed the road to the tavern and took his hat off as he entered. Sally was at the counter as though she'd been expecting him.

"Morning, Joe. Coffee?"

"That'd be great Sally," he said approaching the counter. "Someone been in for breakfast already?" he asked sniffing the hot meat grease air.

"I got a young couple in one of the rooms; they arrived in last night before the worst of the snow."

"I saw them pull up," Joe recalled, "when I was out bringing in some logs for the fire."

"Nice kids; they're newlyweds heading for California." Joe nodded disinterestedly at this as his coffee was put in front of him.

"I don't suppose they know where Maul is?" he said.

"I don't suppose they do," Sally smiled. "No luck so far?"

"I went up there but I don't think he's been there for a long time, much longer ago than the last time he was in town."

"Why do you think that?" Sally asked in surprise.

"The forest all around the house is dead and even the wood of the house looks like it dried out to hollow. There was no sign of him being there for a long time."

"Where else could he be?"

"That's what I'm hoping someone will tell me today." A glimmer in Sally's eye grabbed his attention. "You know something that might help me?" he asked quickly. Sally was surprised and she looked guilty a moment, but of what he could have no idea.

"Actually, now that you say that I remember something alright, something I didn't think of a couple of nights ago when you were in asking."

"Which is?"

"One morning after the last time Maul was in town, I was in the galley here and I chanced to look up the hill and he was standing up by the old mine shaft looking down on the town." Something in her demeanour told him she was not telling the whole of it and he looked at her thoughtfully

"What was he doing up there?"

"I don't know, just standing there."

"Looking at you?"

"Not at first but then he must have felt my eyes on him because he looked down right at me."

"Then what?"

"Then nothing, he went on with his day and I did the same."

"And that's it?"

"I know it's not very exciting, sheriff, but you asked about Maul Thorndean and that's all I got for you." Sally smiled as she spoke; back to her cheerful self.

Joe sipped at his coffee and wondered if it was possible Maul was living in the shaft, or if perhaps, there was an old miner's shack up there that he'd never seen before. If there was, it was something new to go on and he decided to take a walk up that way when he was finished his coffee.

Before he said anything else to Sally, there was a noise from the corridor off the main room and the young couple came through the door carrying their bags.

"Morning," Joe said turning to face them and smiling.

"Morning," they both said and they at once looked very nervous.

"Don't worry, kids, he's not here to inspect your marriage license," Sally laughed. The newlyweds laughed nervously looking from each other to Sally to Joe.

"I'm Sheriff Joe Moorefield," he said leaning over to shake their hands.

"Jarrod; and this is my wife Ava."

"I hear you're heading to California?"

"We sure are," Jarrod said, the idea bringing a huge grin to his face.

"It's a long drive from here," Joe said. "Have you had a mechanic look over the car on your travels?"

"She's a reliable vehicle," Jarrod said.

"All the same, if you want, Jeff across the road is a mechanic."

"Thanks," Jarrod said and Joe took this as a no thanks and decided not to push it any more.

"Well, there's been a lot of snow overnight so the roads will be dangerous to the pass and then down the far side too, I imagine," he said. At this Ava looked at Jarrod, her face filled with terror,

"Dangerous?"

"More dangerous than would usually be the case," Jarrod assured her and looking to Joe said nodding. "I'm sure that's what the sheriff means?" Ava looked at Joe who nodded too.

"Oh I'm not looking to scare you," he said with a smile. "I'm just doing my job. You shouldn't have any trouble getting to the valley on the other side and anyway, I'll be driving that road myself later on today and I can see that you've come to no trouble."

"You see?" Jarrod said and then quickly changed to Sally. "Everything here was fantastic; we'd like to settle up with you if we could?"

"I've yet to take issue with that!" Sally smiled, and she pulled a sheet from the notebook by the bar.

While the couple and Sally settled their business, Joe looked along the bar to the galley window Sally had been talking about. From his viewpoint, all he could see was a couple of yards to the right of the building at a slant. He said goodbye to the couple and once they were out of the room, he asked,

"Do you mind if I come back there and have a quick look out your window?" Sally regarded him for a moment and answered,

"I don't think you'll see him, but be my guest."

Joe got up and went behind the bar — the first one he had seen from the back in his life — and went to the galley. Leaning on the sink he looked up the hill to the small clearing he knew was where the mine entrance had been. It didn't seem so far up as he had supposed but he also knew that it was not a direct walking route to get to it; he would have go around by the lake and come back down on the site from above. This thought made it seem even more unlikely that Maul would be living there; he couldn't imagine the man giving up the high ground.

"I'll go on up and have a look," he said as he walked back out to the customer side of things.

"Well, you see Maul up there you tell him I was asking for him to come back on into town, things are a little dead around for my taste at the moment."

"I'll tell him," Joe said smiling as he placed the money for his coffee and a tip on the counter by his cup.

Half an hour later Joe Moorefield stood outside his office once again. He'd changed some of his clothes and got more supplies for a hike. It wasn't particularly long but with the weather as unpredictable as it was it was probably better to be safe and have more than he needed with him. There was a low breeze as he walked that tossed up the white surface all around and making it look as though there was light snow once more.

Thankfully it stayed fine on the walk up and as he passed the lake (a large pool really but he never got into this point with the locals) he noted that it had partially frozen over. When he'd first come here he recalled the previous sheriff telling him if the lake froze, they were probably in for a harsh time of it. He suspected the pool was fed by a warm spring somewhere within the mountain but didn't know for sure.

Though he was no tracker, Joe could see that there had been movement in the general area of the mine opening. Various animal tracks and droppings were scattered around and there was even one well preserved boot-print in the mud. Joe leaned over to look at it more closely for any giveaway marks on the grips but saw nothing that could help him. As he touched the sides, he found that the hole and print were frozen solid. Standing up he then placed his own boot beside it for comparison. It was roughly the same. He knew that Maul was a couple of inches shorter than he was but he didn't know about the man's shoe-size. It might have been Maul, or it might not; there was no way to tell for sure save checking the underside of Maul's boots the next time he saw him.

From where he stood, Joe could see down to the town. It looked even smaller from up here, more like a farmhouse with a few out buildings than a town. His own little sheriff's office looked smallest of all and it made him wonder why the buildings had been built so small and close to one another.

Turning his attention to the mine entrance, he noticed that the old wooden boards that were nailed down across were rotted and there were some holes at ground level where animals must go in and out. It wasn't big enough for a man, however. Joe tugged gently to see if any of the boards were loose but none were. Maul wasn't living in there, anyway. As he pried like this, he felt the soft of the wood and knew how easily it would come apart in his hands if he wanted it to. There obviously had been little forethought in closing the mine, and Joe supposed it was a blessing that there were no children or teenagers living in Mercy. It would surely be a draw and a death-trap to them!

Just then, his hands felt a different texture, and he looked at the wood. It was dry and hard and white; very familiar to him. He pressed, and the wood shattered and fell down within the shaft. It was the same as the wood all around Maul's place. There was little of it on the planks and Joe spent the next few minutes looking around the clearing for any more evidence of what must be some arboreal disease he'd never heard of. There was little sign but every few feet he would come across some trace but it was always small and didn't seem to be spreading. He wondered if the trees here were perhaps more resilient that at other parts of the forest. Were these marks the last remnants of the disease on this area?

Chapter 11

Ava stood shivering in the cold and looking around nervously as Jarrod pushed the mounds of snow from the car with his hands. There really had been a lot of it overnight and when he was done clearing all the windows, there was a pile almost a foot deep all around. He opened the door — which also took a lot of effort as it had frozen — and then beckoned Ava to get in.

"Let's hope it doesn't take too long to heat up today," she said through chattering teeth as she got in.

"Let's hope," Jarrod echoed. He didn't think it would, but he knew once they were moving Ava would be fine. There were plenty of blankets to keep her warm, and if that didn't do it the excitement of being back on the road might. He sat behind the wheel and pushed the key into the ignition and turned.

A choking noise emitted from the engine but this was not the usual gasps for life Jarrod had become used to before the car would sputter into life. This was a grinding noise he'd never heard before and he worried the end had finally come. Ava looked at him, her smile fading rapidly.

"What is it?" she asked looking to his hands as he turned the key once more.

"It's probably nothing, just the cold," Jarrod said pressing on the accelerator hopefully. That same harsh noise as before filled the car and Ava put her hands to her ears as Jarrod let off the pedal and killed the ignition. "I'll have a look under the hood," he said as cheerily as he could before she could say anything else. He got out and had a time of it trying to get the lid of the hood up. It was both frozen shut and there was so much snow that it weighed a tonne too. At last, he got around these obstacles and he looked at the engine. He could tell there were all sorts of things not right from the first glance. He was no mechanic, but he had looked under here many times before and what he was seeing was not familiar to him at all. He wondered if this much damage — which is what he assumed he was seeing — could have been done in only the last few weeks of pushing the car so much each day to get as far as they could as fast as they could.

Letting the hood drop he shook his head at the expectant face of Ava peering at him through the windshield.

"What is it?" she mouthed, and he walked to her side and opened the door a little,

"I guess we're going to have to look in on that mechanic the sheriff was talking about after all."

"Oh no," Ava groaned.

"Don't worry; I'm sure he'll have it fixed in time. Why don't you go back inside and get a cup of coffee to keep you warm while I go talk to him?"

"No, I'll come with you, I want to hear what he says," Ava said and Jarrod knew that there was going to be no discouraging her out of this.

They trudged over to the store and went inside.

"Hi again," Jeff said from behind his counter.

"Hi," Jarrod said, "We need a mechanic; is that you?"

"Yes it is," Jeff smiled, though he was not best pleased about the prospect of handing frozen metal on a day like this.

"Our car is out front of the tavern, there," Jarrod pointed and Jeff looked out at it, "But it won't start; it's making a strange noise like I never heard from it before."

"It might be just seized up from the cold night we had," Jeff said hopefully, "But I guess we better go out and have a better look."

"Why don't you stay in the store and out of the cold?" Jarrod suggested to Ava. Jeff looked at her with what she perceived as distrust but the man caught himself and smiled, nodding,

"That sounds like a sensible idea to me."

"If it's all the same, I'd like to come out and look with you. I've been developing an interest in how cars run since we came on this trip," Ava said. Jarrod looked at her in surprise and Jeff laughed.

"I guess we'll be having ladies doing all kinds of jobs in the future!" he said leading the way out through the door. Jarrod was still looking at his wife as he went out after her. What was she doing, and why was she so interested in the car all of a sudden? The truth struck home almost as soon as he'd had the thought — she wanted to hear what the mechanic said not Jarrod's own enhanced version. She didn't want to be protected from the truth.

As this idea, he grew nervous as they approached the car. It had looked bad, but he hadn't indicated that to Ava when she asked. It could be a huge job after all; the car might even be at the end of the road considering what he saw under the hood. He opened up the hood and put the rod in place to hold it up."

"Holy shit!" Jeff exclaimed and then looking at Ava and covering his mouth said, "Pardon me ma'am." Jarrod's heart sank at the reaction and he could bring himself to look at Ava for fear of seeing either tears or anger in them.

"What is it?" Jarrod asked of Jeff. The mechanic looked at him as if in disbelief,

"All these wires and cables have been torn out," he said, "This was done deliberately!"

"Deliberately!" Ava said, a bolus of fear choking up her windpipe as she gripped Jarrod's arm.

"Who would do such a thing?" Jarrod said dumbfounded, "Out here?" he added as if to emphasize the oddity of it.

"The person who was at the window last night!" Ava said, and she started to cry.

"Someone was at your window?" Jeff parroted, and he looked around the place. It was clear that he was just as uneasy with what had happened to the car as the young couple were.

"She thought she saw someone..."

"I know what I saw," Ava interrupted Jarrod. "But I let you convince me it was my imagination!"

"Who was it?" Jeff asked looking to her.

"How would I know who it was?" she answered indignantly.

"You didn't recognise him then? He wasn't anyone who was in the tavern last night?"

"I don't know, it was late and dark outside, it was hard to make him out," Ava said as though in apology for her lack of focus at the time, and then turning swiftly on Jarrod said, "But I know there was someone there!" Jarrod felt at a loss,

"I don't understand any of this," he said.

"We better talk to the sheriff about this," Jeff said.

"Who do you think it was?" Ava suddenly asked him.

"I have no idea, but there's only one person who I can imagine doing something like this to a stranger's car."

"Who?"

"Maul Thorndean."

"The animal you were all trying to scare us about?" Jarrod asked. Jeff nodded guiltily to this question.

"He's never done anything like this before," he said, "but I just can't see any way that it could be anyone else."

Jeff had only taken one step away from the car when Ava asked,

"How long would it take you to fix the car?" Jeff looked at her and then at Jarrod before peering back down into the damaged engine.

"I don't have most of those cables in stock. I'd have to order from Emerson and it could be two days before they came up here."

"Two days!"

"I'm sorry, this is not a usual problem, normally those wires and cables are replaced long before they are too damaged but this is wholesale destruction."

"What are we supposed to do?" she asked.

"I suppose you'll have to stay here at the tavern until I can fix your car," he shrugged. Jarrod put his arms around Ava and pulled her close to him.

"Can you go ring for the parts now and we will go tell the sheriff about the car?" he suggested to Jeff.

"Fine," Jeff said, and he walked off back towards his store.

"Why would someone do this to us?" Ava asked through her tears as she buried her face in Jarrod's shoulder.

"I don't know, Ava, but don't worry, we'll let the sheriff know, and then we will be safe here until the car is ready. We'll leave the very second it's fixed, night or day, I promise."

"I don't want to be here," Ava said, "Maybe the sheriff, or that mechanic will drive us to Emerson?"

"I'll ask," Jarrod assured her and hugged her tighter than ever. "I'll ask."

There was no answer when they got to the sheriff's office but the door was open. Inside there was a notepad and pencil handing on a string on the wall that said: Leave a message here and I'll get to you as soon as I see it — Sheriff Moorefield.

"Write something," Ava said. Jarrod picked up the pencil and poised it over the paper.

"What will I say?" Ava didn't have a suggestion but only nodded back to the paper like they were in some dire hurry. Jarrod paused another moment and then wrote:

Dear Sheriff Moorefield, Can you please contact Jarrod in the Tavern when you get this message. Someone has done damage to our car. Regards, Jarrod.

"Shouldn't you put your surname on it?" Ava asked as they left.

"I don't think he'll be confused as to who it's from."

When then came out, Jeff was back on the street and he waved them over when he saw them.

"The sheriff in there?" he asked.

"No, we left a note though."

"He might be in the tavern having some coffee," Jeff said.

"I don't think so; he was in there earlier and has left since."

"Did you get to order the parts?" Ava asked.

"No, I didn't get an answer, but I'll try again in a few minutes. Don't worry I'll get them ordered today."

"Do you think you could drive us into Emerson?" Ava asked. Jeff looked very surprised at this request and he shook his head before talking.

"No, I couldn't do that, I have the store here to look after and someone else might need a mechanic too."

"Come on," Jarrod said taking Ava by the hand. "We should check back into the tavern." This wasn't what she wanted to hear; she only wanted to be out of this town, but she knew at that moment that there was no other option.

Chapter 12

Mouse Allen stumbled out of the Lone Wolf Tavern into the blustery night. Two things happened when the cold air shocked into his body; first, he suddenly felt much more drunk than when he decided he was going home, and second, he felt he needed to pee. Badly. His car was only a few yards away, so he decided to go and take a quick leak behind it rather than go back inside and have Sally mock him about coming back to use the toilet.

Taking the leak didn't prove to be so easy, however, and the cold weather coupled with his bulky coat made things difficult and he ended up peeing a little on his leg.

"Fuck!" he griped through gritted teeth shaking his leg out and trying to make sure no more hit him. He looked back to the tavern as he re-buckled and was glad to see no one about who might have witnessed this. He climbed into the truck and turned on the ignition. It started as well as ever and he reversed out from the building without a glance behind. It was late and the chances of hitting someone were so slim he rarely looked at all when he was like this.

Angling the car towards his home a mile down the hill, he let it roll for a bit before kicking it into gear again. He liked the feeling of the free rolling heaviness under him, especially when he'd had a few too many beers. It gave him a sense of power, inexplicably, that he could feel at no other time during his week.

Mouse saw the white car of the young couple and he recalled hearing from Jeff how badly damaged it had been, and how Joe had been in asking if anyone knew where Maul was living now. Everyone, save Sally, thought it could only have been Maul who had done this to the car, and the girl, Ava, had said he had been peeking in at her before bed as well. The sooner the better Joe found him and arrested him for this.

He was so busy thinking on these things and looking at the white car that he let his own slide further than usual and it took a huge swerve while getting the car into gear at the same time to stop him caroming right into the steps of the sheriff's office. He laughed with relief as he got control and slowed on down the hill.

"That would have taken some explaining," he laughed looking back out the rear window as the town receded.

The road was like a black tunnel ahead with white borders all around it. Small flutters of snow falling looked like they were coming at him from within the darkness and he liked seeing them splash lightly into the windshield and slide down.

Mouse got to his home in only a few minutes and he slowed to take the awkward angle of his driveway. As he did this movement caught his eyes, and he looked to something rushing fast from the side of his house.

"What the..." He crashed the car into a picket fence that ran over his lawn and pressed hard on the brake as the car juddered and splintering wood filled his ears. "Fuck. What a night!" he said. In his shock at hitting the fence, he had forgotten for a moment what had caused it, but then the image flooded back into his mind and scared him. He looked all about but could see nothing. Had it been a man? That had been his first idea, but the body shape that hung in his memory didn't hold up to that idea. It looked like a man, but it didn't feel to Mouse that it had in fact been a man.

Peering into the dark of the woods that surrounded his house from three sides he could make no sense of anything out. Everything looked different to him, like this was somewhere entirely new to him, but he had been in this house since he was a child and knew every inch of his land. Still, nothing looked like it had when he left here only six hours ago to go to the tavern. What was it? He got out of the car and took a deep breath of the cold air hoping it would go some way towards unblurring his vision a little. He closed his eyes and kneaded them with his fists and then looked around again. Everything looked white that was it. Was there snow stuck to the bark of all the trees? He didn't recall seeing much of that before.

He walked towards the house, looking around nervously as he went. He'd seen something, of that he was in no doubt, but the fact that he didn't know what he had seen made him fearful. It was so white everywhere, even with all the snow it shouldn't be this white, it was throwing off his concentration, stopping him from thinking rationally about what he should do which was getting his gun. He stumbled towards the side of the house where he had seen the thing and he noticed then that the trees closest to the house were not covered in snow like he'd thought. They were white and grey and looked like they had been long dead, scorched by the fire of many decades past. It was dead wood, rampike, but that made little sense at all. It would take years for this kind of damage to show up, and that was only after a fire. Nothing had happened out here where he lived, least of all a fire. All around him, these dead trees stood like silent soldiers looking down on him. He began to feel uneasy like he really was under their gaze and scrutiny. This time he did rush into the house.

Going straight to his gun cabinet he took out his rifle, assured himself it was loaded and cocked it. Then he stood there silent and listening on the off chance that he wasn't alone in the house. He knew the house to be of old wood and there was not a chance of anything moving without his knowing about it. When no creaking came for a long time, he went to the window and looked outside into the forest again. The dead trees were everywhere. He watched for movement but saw nothing in any direction.

At last, he mustered up the courage to go back outside and went to the side of the house where the intruder had been. He intended to see the footprints to confirm this. What he saw instead was nothing he could put a name to. There were markings all over the snow but nothing he could call a footprint. Tiny lines scratched the surface all over and it looked like the snow had been gathered up like with a sweeping brush. In fact, now that he thought about it, it reminded him of the tracks left in the snow when a Christmas tree was pulled through it. What could it mean?

With his gun cocked, he walked a few steps into the darkness and looked at the ground. It looked something similar, but the terrain was getting more uneven with each step and it was hard to tell in this dark where the track might lead. Mouse decided that he would need the torch he kept in the trunk of the car for this job. He crumped back out to his driveway and walked along to the diagonally abandoned car. Just as he got to the truck, however, he lost his footing, slipped and banged his head hard on the rear fender of the car. He slumped to the ground and groaned, putting his hand to his head and feeling the slick of blood there. He tried to pull himself back up but found he didn't have the strength for this and instead slid further down until he was on his back on the snow. For a few moments, he looked to the sky, seeing his own shallowing breaths rise above him. Something was moving nearby, something in the trees but he couldn't turn to look; there was no power left in his body. He was terrified but even that was only a feeling as if from far away, like from another time. He tried to speak but nothing came from his mouth and then he slipped into the darkness of unconsciousness.

Chapter 13

It was still dark when Sheriff Joe Moorefield was rudely awoken by the persistent hammering on his door. He sat bolt up and looked around, confused for a moment as to what was going on. Someone was knocking on the outer door of the office; and that meant something must have happened.

"I'm coming!" he called out as he jumped out of bed and got dressed. No one had ever called on him like this before and he could only assume the worst. Someone was dead; there had been an accident or a fight of some kind. What else could be so urgent? The knocking had stopped but now Joe could hear the sounds of heavy footsteps as the person on the planks outside paced up and down.

"Who's out there, anyway?" Joe called putting on his watch and nothing the time of 3.22am.

"It's me, Mouse," the voice came back. It sounded like he was chattering through cold but Joe didn't notice that it was all that cold compared to lately. He went to the door and opened it to see Mouse standing there shivering and with damp bloodstain matted on his face and head.

"What happened to you?" Joe asked in surprise.

"There's someone down at my house, sheriff," Mouse answered, "you have to come look."

"Who is it?" Joe asked stepping out of the house and closing the door behind him.

"I don't know, but we got to go see." Mouse was rushing back off and Joe saw then that he had come on foot.

"Where's your car?" he asked,

"Back home," Mouse answered looking at him as if it was a very strange question to ask. Joe walked up to Mouse and took him by the arm to have a closer look at his head.

"I think we should go inside and get this cleaned up before we do anything else," he said.

"No, we need to get going; they'll get away if we delay any more."

"Mouse, you've come all the way from your house on foot, if they are looking to escape they will be long gone by now. Was it someone burglarizing your house?"

"I'm not sure; I think I disturbed them when I came home."

"Let's get you cleaned up," Joe suggested again.

"No, I can do that when I get home," Mouse insisted and Joe saw there was no point in trying to argue with him. He was both drunk—by the smell of him—and probably concussed by the gash on his head.

"What were you hit with?" he asked.

"I don't know," Mouse answered in impatience. "Can we just get going?"

"Alright, Mouse, take it easy," Joe said, and he unlocked the jeep and they both got in.

They were at the house in only a few minutes and Joe saw at once the car crashed up over the lawn and the smashed fence,. He looked at Mouse but the large man jumped out of the car as soon as it had come to a halt and was waiting eagerly for Joe to follow him.

As Joe got out of the jeep, he looked around for any telltale signs in the snow and his eyes landed on a rifle underneath the car. He bent down to pick it up and as he did he saw blood on the fender and ground there, and also the marks that might be made by someone slipping on the snow.

"Is this your rifle?" he asked holding it up for Mouse to see. Mouse looked at it and then a confused look came over his face.

"It is," he said and Joe could tell he didn't remember having it before.

"So what happened here, Mouse," Joe asked nodding to the car.

"I came home and just as I was about to pull into the drive, I saw someone coming from the side of the house."

"And that made you lose control and crash the car?"

"Yeah, I was trying to see who it was and didn't realise the car was still moving."

"You're pretty drunk, Mouse," Joe said with a sceptical look on his face. "Are you sure you didn't just imagine seeing someone?" Mouse's face turned red with indignation, but Joe didn't see this. Just as he had been asking the last question, he had noticed the white of the trees all around and a sense of fear came into him once more.

"I swear to you, Joe, I saw someone!" Mouse said. Joe wasn't listening, he was thinking back a couple of days past when he knew for sure that he had passed by this house on his way in to Emerson. There had definitely been no sign of this damage to the trees then.

"When did the trees go like this?" he asked Mouse. Mouse looked around and it was like a switch went of his head and he was seeing it again having noticed it himself earlier.

"I saw that too when I got home, it wasn't like that when I was leaving to go to the tavern this evening." Though he sounded as sure as could be, Joe scoffed at this.

"You want me to believe all of this happened while you were in town for a few hours?"

"I'm telling you the truth!"

"Mouse, look at the fender of the car here, and this slip mark and then your outline in the snow," Joe said pointing. Mouse looked down, and then back to him and shrugged. "You slipped and banged your head and were knocked out just here. That's when you dropped your rifle under there!"

"I don't remember that," Mouse admitted. "But come over here and look at this!" he said running to the side of the house and beckoning the sheriff to follow. Joe sighed, thinking of how tired he would be all day tomorrow now that he had been dragged from his sleep on a wild goose chase. He walked over to where Mouse was now standing and looked down to where he was pointing.

"What's this supposed to be?" Joe asked wearily. He could see the ground was criss-crossed with markings but none he could identify.

"That's from whatever was here; this is what ran from the side of the house." Joe looked at it again and then looked up to Mouse who was staring back at him expectantly.

"This is nothing," he said, "nothing at all."

"It's tracks from something," Mouse insisted. On seeing that Joe was still not impressed, he said, "Wait here a second." Joe stood as Mouse hurried back to the car and looked around on the ground. After about thirty seconds, there was a sound of triumph and he came back with a torch with the light beaming at the ground. "I was just starting to follow the tracks earlier when I got distracted, I think." Joe took the torch and looked at the markings on the ground. It was true that it looked like it was moving in the one direction but it still didn't look like any tracks Joe had ever seen. Walking into the trees, he scanned the ground and saw that it seemed to be leading away from the house as Mouse had said. It got harder to see clearly in the choppy ground within the tree line but Joe managed to follow it until it came to an abrupt end at the trunks of one of the trees. From here, there was no more trace of it. The only thing he could imagine was whoever or whatever it was must have climbed a tree and he ran the light up the trunk and into the branches above. There were signs of damage to the limbs up there but that when he scanned around with the torchlight, it was the same in all the other trees. It was this new white weakness that seemed to break so easily.

"What the hell is all this white on the trees, anyway?" he asked aloud.

"It looks like rampike," Mouse said, "but I've never seen it like this and I never knew it as a thing that could spread either."

"Rampike?" Joe said; he'd never heard the word before but was glad that it had one.

"Yeah," Mouse nodded. "It's dead wood, normally been killed by fire or struck by lightning, but this is very strange and there sure hasn't been any fires or lightning around here lately."

"This is happening all over the mountain," Joe said. "Maul's house is completely surrounded by this stuff and even his house is damaged by it."

"It was probably him who I saw here tonight," Mouse said bitterly.

"What makes you think that?"

"The reason I think it was him who damaged that couple's car; who else could it be?"

"We can't go around making assumptions like that with no proof," Joe said, but even he thought it very odd that all of this was going on at the same time that Maul Thorndean was missing.

"Well, you tell me who else then?" Mouse asked.

"I don't know who else," Joe said. "But I've nothing in my mind pointing towards Maul at this point."

"So what are you going to do about this?" Mouse asked indicating his land with his hands.

"I will come back here in the morning and have a look in the daylight. Until then, I think you should get yourself cleaned up and then get some sleep. Don't come out here and disturb the place until I come out, do you hear me?"

"Yeah, yeah," Mouse said.

"And you need to stop driving home drunk, too," Joe said nodding back to the car. Mouse nodded grumpily in agreement but didn't respond verbally.

As Joe pulled away from the house and did a U-turn in the jeep. He scoured the land that was lit up in the headlights and wondered what, if anything, had been going on here tonight. Mouse seemed adamant that he had seen someone and there were marks to indicate that someone, perhaps dragging something behind them had been here. Then again, Mouse had been very drunk, so drunk in fact that he had managed to fall and knock himself out for a time. It was hard to know what to think. In the morning, he would be able to see the area better; Mouse would be sober and perhaps better able to know if he did see anything, and he would also be able to tell if anything was missing from the house. Joe just hoped he might get at least one more hour of sleep in before it was time to start another day.

Chapter 14

The light of the morning sun reflected off the glass of Susan Bloom's windscreen as she made her way over the high roads that would lead soon back to Mercy. There was still snow all around, but clear skies glowed now and the world looked as about as beautiful as possible. The white powder lay everywhere, on the ground, roads and every limb of every tree and it sparkled in the sun like exotic jewellery.

The road rose and dropped in front of her, making sections in the near distance invisible until cresting the hillocks before those sections. About two miles out from Mercy, Susan noticed on one of the rises that there was something large in the road ahead. It disappeared and reappeared a few times before she finally got the sense of what it might be. Whatever it was large, but not a tree— she didn't think so, anyway. It was dark in colour. A couple of rises out she finally saw that it was a felled deer and as she got closer saw that it was a big steer. It would have taken a lot to take this guy down. She pulled up about twenty feet from the prostrated animal and looked at it for a few moments.

It wasn't moving and there was some blood at its rear legs and on the ground behind. She wasn't sure if it was dead or not. There was room to go around it if she was careful but she was too curious and after a few minutes, she got out of the car and looked at it from a closer vantage. The animal was huge and apart from the blood on its hindquarters, the fur all over looked slick with sweat — like a horse after a race. She took a step closer to try to have a look at the animal's face but just as she moved, the whole body twitched and the legs jerked into the air for a moment. Susan let out a shriek of surprise and stood rigid to the spot. She was very suddenly aware that this creature had the capability of killing her even in its injured state — perhaps even more likely to kill her in this state. Thick plumes of mist rose from the mouth and nostrils as it breathed heavily.

The head rested back on the cold hard road and Susan felt very sorry for the deer despite her fear. She looked once more at the injuries and wondered how a car could have done that and yet leave no trace of the car anywhere she could see. As far as she was aware, there were no predators capable of taking down a stag deer in this mountain range. The thought came to her of putting the dying animal out of its misery but there was no method coming to mind that she had either the stomach or capability of carrying out.

"Who did this to you?" she whispered and then took a step back in fright at the head snapping in her direction at the sound of her voice. No sooner had this happened, however, than the stag flopped down flat and went completely limp and motionless. Susan stood and stared at it for a long time, wondering if it had died but at the same time scared that it had not.

As it always did with Susan, her curiosity got the better of her fear and she took another tentative step forward.

"You still alive?" she asked in her normal speaking voice. This time there was no sign of awareness on the stricken deer's part. She stamped her feet and still no reaction came. Now she walked a few steps closer, making noise as she did so. Her eyes moved from the ribs to the head looking for signs of breathing but no movement or vapour came to vision.

When close enough, Susan moved in a large arc so that she could come around to the stag head on and see its face. When at last she could see the eyes were wide open, but it was clear that there was no life in them. A great pang of sadness came over Susan and she walked the last few feet and fell to her knees at the huge head of the magnificent animal. Tears came to her eyes as she stroked the still warm cheeks, the fur soft and silky to her touch. She looked over his hulking frame, her eyes falling once more on the injuries that had crippled it and then saw something that surprised her. There was long stakes of wood, not stakes exactly, not formed like stakes but sharp sticks maybe, jutting out from the bloodied wounds.

"How did you do that?" she asked thinking now that this had been some freak accident involving only the deer and a splintered tree trunk. She looked into the woods where the deer must have come from but could see no evidence of the tree that caused this. Was it possible these wooden spikes were the only loose ones on the tree until the collision, and the stag had then taken them all away with him in his unstoppable motion?

The wounds looked so painful; certainly a horrible way to die. Susan supposed she should tell the sheriff about it when she got back to Mercy. The animal would have to be moved off the road at the very least. She imagined the whole town could be fed for a couple of weeks with the meat if it was dressed properly. Though she liked deer meat, somehow this animal didn't seem all that appealing given the injuries she was seeing close up. She knew that a bullet didn't leave a pleasant wound either but she didn't normally see what her dinner looked like just after it had been killed.

A rustling in the thicket caught her ear, and she looked into the trees. There was nothing, but she wondered was it perhaps the mate of this fallen stag. Susan felt eyes on her but couldn't locate them. That same fear as before came over her and she stood up, preparing to run back to her car if need be. Another noise, rustling and like twigs breaking at the same time. Still she saw no movement.

"Hello?" she called out, more out of scared instinct than anything else. Silence answered her. The feeling of unease moved her body back a step but she was still facing the trees where the sound had come from. Her heart pounded, and all she wanted right then was to be in her car and on her way home.

A thunderous crash resounded in the air and Susan looked in horror as what seemed like a huge scraggly bush came bounding at her across the snow. She screamed and turned to run losing her footing a moment and going down on one hand and knee. Scurrying forward in panic she got back to her feet but still was slipping as she tried to run away.

Whatever it was behind her was sliding and scratching all over the icy road and she could only hope it went down hard and was unable to get up long enough for her to get the car. The door was still open and the key in the ignition waiting for her.

A ferocious growl came from so close she jumped in ever deeper fear than before and then felt the hard slam of huge weight into her side. Her ribs ached, and the wind was knocked from her lungs and the pain and feeling of not breathing terrified her. She felt weightless, and it took a split second for her to realise she was no longer on the ground. The air spun around her and she felt her stomach churn as she went head over heels and landed heavily in the woody debris-filled ditch on the opposite side of the road.

Laying there, all Susan could do was look up into the sky and hope some air would some back into her lungs before the animal came on her again. Tears were streaming down her cheeks, hot like flowing lava it seemed, but though the breath was returning to her, it was shockingly painful to draw it.

Whatever had attacked her was out of sight, back up on the road but she could hear it moving around. It shuffled back and forth like something agitated and the growls though low were menacing in tone. Each scrape of the ground brought new terror to her as she though it would appear at the edge of the ditch and look down hungrily at her before pouncing down and finishing her off.

For what seemed like a very long time, noises came from the road above her. The sounds were muffled in her snow packed ears and though she could understand the growling from time to time, nothing else made sense to her. After a time in which she felt she must have passed out for a couple of minutes, she came to notice that there was no more noise. She was conscious now and painfully raising one arm to clear the snow from her face and head, she tilted her head to listen better.

Many minutes passed like this and only the quiet of the forest met her ears. A deep sigh escaped painfully as she felt safe — safe from an imminent bad end, anyway. There was still the matter of her badly injured body; she didn't know how badly but she knew damn sure she had never felt this pained in her entire life. She'd broken her leg as a teenager but this felt much worse than that and she was having trouble breathing comfortably. She needed to try get back to the car; she didn't know if she would be able to drive or not, but she also knew that lying here in this ditch would not be doing her body any favours.

Susan looked up the embankment and was glad at least that it was not too high, only about seven feet. She could do this, she was sure of it. Gritting her teeth, she moved on to her front. The pain was so incredibly sharp that she let out a fresh scream and black spots appeared in her visions; she was sure she would pass out again.

"Goddamn!" she said when finally she was able to. At least she had completed the turn, however, and she was now on her belly on the slope. Over the next hour, with frequent and increasingly long breaks, she slowly made her way to the crest.

At last, her head topped the rise and she let it fall heavily to the snow bank to rest. She felt both euphoric and heavily drowsy at the same time. From her new vantage, she could see the road once more; her car waiting as she had left it so it would seem. Her eyes drew back to the stag, and she was shocked to see that it was no longer there. Whatever had come at her must have taken it away. Was that why she had been attacked in the first place? Did some animal think she was trying to steal its dinner? She certainly hoped so and the relief this brought to her, along with the agonizing pain and effort she had made combined to exhaust her and Susan fell asleep on the roadside in the snow.

Chapter 15

On that same morning, Jeff was traveling back from Emerson too. He'd become so annoyed at Ava's pleading eyes every time he went into the tavern, that he had decided to go to get the parts needed for the car and get them on their way, rather than wait for the delivery to Mercy as he would have normally. He hadn't stopped grumbling about the trip all the way there and now he was at the same again on his way back. In his head, he was calculating all the gas he was using, and he would put that, plus a premium, on the young couple's bill for his hardships. He intended to drink his few beers in peace tonight; with no one looking forlornly at him wanting work done he wasn't in a position to get done yet.

Glancing at his watch, he saw the trip had taken him longer than he'd both hoped and planned. The store was closed and by now it was possible he was missing customers — it didn't matter that they had nowhere else to shop and that they would be back later when they saw he was open; Jeff always considered a delayed sale as being the same as a lost sale. Perhaps he should stick an estimate of this on their bill too, he thought.

Not much farther up the road, Jeff saw that someone was parked pretty much in the middle of the lane.

"What's this stupidity, now?" he wondered. He couldn't make out the car yet but he imagined it would be a roadside fix for him to have to do. This was the last thing he needed today.

As he got closer, he was able to see that it was Susan Bloom's car. Jeff liked Susan, and had been friends with her father before he passed away. The door on the driver side was open, but he didn't see her standing around anywhere. He wondered with a childish smile if she had been caught short and had darted into the trees to relieve herself. Her cheeks would be brightly blazing when she came out and saw him if that was the case. Jeff slowed up and came to a halt behind Susan's car and looked around once more. He decided he would give her a minute to appear before he got out and called out to her.

When a more than sufficient time to answer a call of nature elapsed, Jeff thought something might not be right here. It wasn't all that far to town from here after all; surely if she needed to use the bathroom, she would have waited until she got home. He stepped out of his car and called out,

"Susan?" No answer came, and he looked around for any sign of her. Leaning back into the car he honked the horn a couple of time and then stood up and waited a moment to see if this would bring her from whatever was holding her up. After a minute it was clear she was not coming.

Jeff walked over to her car and looked inside; it was empty, and the key was still in the ignition though the engine was not ticking over. He went to the front of the vehicle and felt the hood. It was warm, but not very. The engine had been killed a few hours past by now. This was worrying, but he tried not to think the worst; it was possible she'd had some engine trouble and was now walking back to town. And the door open and the key in the ignition? His mind asked. She rushed off and forgot, he thought, but it didn't sound likely. His eyes wandered to the ground searching out the footprints that would show Susan had walked towards town. They were there alright, but as he followed them absently, he was confronted with a massive smudged red slush of snow that could only be blood!

Before knowing why, or even what he was doing, Jeff ran over and stood at the spot looking down. There was no mistaking it was blood. Was it Susan's? Instinctively he called out her name again, and he heard the infused panic in his own voice. He looked around and felt the horrible beating of his pounding heart in his chest as true fear took over. What the hell had happened here? He looked back to his own car parked behind Susan's and it seemed like it couldn't be farther away.

In this fearful state, his mind turned to his gun which was under his seat in the car. Without thinking anymore he ran, his eyes darting all over for some attack that might originate from any direction. In this frantic spinning of head and roving of eyes something familiar caught his eye, and he looked a moment longer at the mound of snow on the opposite side of the road. For a moment, he didn't know what he was seeing at all but slowly it came to him. It was a person; a woman lying there in the snow. It was Susan!

Jeff stopped in his run and slid but at the same time had the thought that something bad had happened here and that perhaps the gun might still be required. He shuffled on the rest of the way, got it out and looked around once more before going back to where Susan lay.

The first thing that struck him, apart from the fact she was unconscious, was how little blood was on her. There was a gash on her head and some cuts about her, but nothing that could explain even a sixteenth of the blood that was on the road.

"Susan, are you alright? Can you hear me? It's Jeff!" he said as he shook her first gently and then a little harder on getting no response. He leaned in and listened at her back and he could hear her heart was beating. It was slow and weak but it was there. Still feeling fearful at not knowing what had happened here, he looked around to make sure nothing, or no one was stalking up on him.

"We better get you to Sally," he said looking over Susan's arms and legs for any sign of obvious breakages. He didn't want to do any more damage to her in the move. He thought for a second of going back to town and bringing help here but who knew how long Susan had been lying in this snow; he had to get her indoors and warmed up as soon as possible. He ran back over to his car and opened the back door where he planned to put her. His eyes darted everywhere, and he knew that he had never been so afraid in his life. He rushed back to Susan and picked her up — not as easy a task as he had anticipated and then struggled back to the car, ready at any moment for the possibility he would have to drop her and cock the rifle if whatever had attacked her came back. Thankfully, in the end, this was unnecessary and nothing came from the shadows to kill him.

Just as Jeff was about to drive away he saw Susan's still open door and thought of the keys in the ignition. Should he get them, he wondered, but his fear answered very clearly no, you should not! He put his foot hard on the pedal and the back of the car swerved on the ice as he took off back towards Mercy.

The two miles of winding bumping road had never seemed so long in all of Jeff's life. He leaned back from time to time to tap Susan on the face or shake her, and he spoke loudly to her all the way. He was very afraid that she would die before he got her to town.

"C'mon Susan!" he shouted back just as Mercy came into view.

As Jeff drove past the sheriff's office he peered in but was moving too fast to see if Moorefield was there or not — he didn't think so as the jeep was not parked outside. A puff of snow went up in the air as Jeff pulled to a sharp halt outside the Lone Wolf Tavern.

"Sally!" he called out as he got out and opened the back door to take Susan out. "Sally!"

"What's all the hollering about?" Sally's gruff voice came from behind him a moment later. Everything in her jocular facade changed when she saw the bloodied head of Susan Bloom loll in Jeff's arms as he pulled her from the car.

"What happened?" Sally cried.

"I don't know; I found her like this out on the Emerson road," Jeff said pushing against Sally to get her to move towards the tavern. Taking the hint Sally turned and held open the door.

"Get her inside, down to one of the rooms," she said.

Sally rushed around him and opened the door to the short hall of rooms, looking at Susan and happy at least to see that she was breathing as Jeff moved her around laboriously.

"She was out on the road, alone?" Sally asked not having gotten her head around that idea.

"Her car was parked in the middle of the road and she was lying in the ditch like this," Jeff said clearly struggling for breath.

"Set her down on the bed," Sally said as they entered one of the rooms. "As gently as you can," she added, afraid he would just drop her in his exhaustion.

"Susan!" a new voice entered and both Jeff and Sally turned in surprise to see Sam rushing in through the door. He'd seen them come into the tavern as he was coming back into town from working this morning. "Susan!" he said again pushing past the two of them to get to her side. Jeff and Sally looked at one another and it was clear that neither of them thought feelings could run this deep between the two younger people. As far as anyone knew there was nothing going on between them.

"Take is easy, Sam," Sally said trying to ease him back from the bedside. "I need to take a look."

"What can you do for her?" Sam asked shrugging her hands from him.

"Sally was a nurse before she came to town," Jeff said calmly. "She's the only one of us here who can possibly do anything." Sam looked up at Jeff as though to assess if he was telling the truth and then reluctantly made way for Sally.

Sally quickly leaned in and two men watched as she ran her hand over Susan's body and then looked more carefully at the head wound. After a few minutes she stood back up,

"I'll go get some water and clean her up."

"Is she going to be alright?" Sam asked.

"Feels like a couple of broken ribs and hopefully only a concussion."

"Hopefully?"

"Yes, I hope that's why she's unconscious because if it's not it could be a lot worse," Sally said almost angrily. Then in a lighter voice said, "I'll strap up her ribs and wash her cuts and hopefully she'll come round when she's more comfortable." Sam looked appalled at this and Jeff took him by the arm,

"I'm sure Susan will be fine, Sam," he said. "Let's get out of Sally's way and let her do what's needed." This time, Sam did not resist the hands that were on him and with one last forlorn look at Susan he let himself be led from the room.

"Don't worry, Sam," Sally said. "I'm good at this stuff."

"Let's go get ourselves a drink," Jeff said, and he saw that his hands were shaking. He was very glad that his main responsibility in this matter was at an end.

"Go take what you want from the bar," Sally said, and she went down the hall to get the water and supplies she would need for Susan.

Chapter 16

Sheriff Joe Moorefield pulled up outside the office having been up at the Thorndean place again this morning. He'd been looking for more signs of Maul, clambering through the limbs of the trees to see if there was any sign of accident around the place. It made no sense at all that Maul would have just disappeared knowing how fiercely he valued the land he owned, even with the overrun of trees.

As Joe got out of the car, he noticed that Jeff Sorkin's vehicle was parked outside the tavern which was unusual; he never parked anywhere other than at his house behind the store on the other side of the wide road. It was odd, but it wasn't enough to warrant Joe going down to find out why; he was sure there would be some easy explanation. He was probably working on the young couple's car and parked close so as not to have to lift parts across the street.

Going into the office, however, he was arrested by the sight of a scrawled note on his out of office notepad. He pulled the clipboard from its hook to look at the writing more clearly. He couldn't be fully sure but he thought it said: Susan attacked. In Tavern. Hurt Badly. Joe tossed the board onto the desk and rushed out for the tavern at once.

When he entered he saw Sam Brainard and Jeff sitting up at the bar, and the first thing he noticed about them was that they were both drinking what looked like whiskey. It was still early in the morning for that and Joe felt a sick feeling come over him knowing that whatever had happened was bad. Sam turned to look at him as he came in and the young man's face was white and sickly looking.

"She's down the hall, there," Jeff said standing up and pointing. Joe nodded and decided to go to Susan first before asking anyone questions.

When he got into the hall, he saw there was one door slightly ajar and assuming this is where she would be he tapped gently. Sally appeared almost at once and looked at him in surprise.

"Is Susan alright?" Joe asked.

"She's not as bad as I thought when she first came in; she came to a few minutes ago, but she's out cold again now." As she spoke, Sally made way for him to come into the room and see Susan for himself. There were damp towels on the floor and he could see blood on some of them but not a whole amount.

"What happened?" he asked on seeing Susan looking much better than he had feared.

"We don't know," Sally said. "Jeff found her on the Emerson back road lying in the road unconscious and bleeding."

"It looks like you did a great job on her," he said looking approvingly at the dressing on Susan's head and noting her tightly wrapped torso. "Looks like you might have had to sacrifice a sheet or two there."

"They were the only things I had for the job; she's got a couple of broken ribs, maybe even three." Joe grimaced the pain this must have caused Susan.

"She didn't say anything when she woke up?"

"No, she just looked around like she was very frightened for a moment and then seemed to calm as she saw she was indoors and I was here." Joe nodded.

"I better go out and talk to Jeff and see what he can tell me. I think it best you give the medical centre in Emerson a call and get them to send an ambulance for Susan just in case." Sally nodded at this.

Sam almost jumped on Joe as soon as he came back into the main room of the tavern.

"Is she any better?" he asked eagerly.

"She is doing better, Sam, now steady on. She woke up for a minute but she's sleeping now. Sally is taking care of her for now and an ambulance will come and take her later on today." Before Sam could say anything else, Joe walked over to Jeff. "What happened, Jeff?"

"I don't know, sheriff," Jeff said looking perplexed. "I came across her car in the road but she wasn't in it and the door was wide open. I thought perhaps she was having engine trouble, so I got out to take a look and that's when I saw the blood all over the ground."

"Blood?" Joe prompted him to go on.

"Yes, there was so much of it that I was frightened right off." This didn't make sense to Joe having seen Susan, but he thought perhaps any amount of blood might seem like a lot to someone not used to it.

"So, where was Susan? On the road?"

"No, she was in the ditch, I only saw her when I was going back to my car for my gun."

"Why did you need your gun?"

"Because of all the blood; I thought something terrible had happened to her."

"Then you saw her and what happened?"

"I went over and saw that she was alive but in a bad way. It was then that I knew all the blood could not have been hers." This alarmed Joe.

"Then whose blood was it?" he asked.

"I don't know; there were markings all over the snow but I couldn't tell for sure what they were. Maybe Susan hit an animal, and it was bleeding but not dead, and when she went to look it could have kicked her and then run off into the woods. That's the best sense I've been able to make of it in my head, anyway."

"Where was this?" Joe asked; he was going to have to go out and have a look at the site himself.

"Not far, maybe three miles but I think less," Jeff answered.

"Nothing else happened? You didn't see anything else I might need to know?" Joe asked. Jeff thought for a moment and then shook his head assuredly.

"No, but wait, I'll come out there with you. We still don't know what did this to her for sure," Jeff said. Joe's immediate instinct was to say no, but he had the feeling that another pair of eyes mightn't be so much of a bad thing out there on that lonely road.

"You better come in my jeep then, if you've been drinking," Joe said looking at the drained glasses on the counter.

Sam had wandered over to where Joe and Jeff were talking and he looked stunned. The door to the hall opened again and Sam bounded back over to meet Sally as she came out.

"Anything new?" he said.

"No," Sally said irritably. "The phone isn't working back there; I'm just going to try the tavern one."

The three watched as she went in behind the bar and lifted the handle from the cradle of the wall mounted telephone. She listened, and the pressed the button a few times and then spun the dial a couple of times for good measure.

"This one's down too," she said looking at Joe. He looked to Jeff.

"Come on over to your store," he said. "I'll make the call from there." Jeff nodded and started for the door. "I'll call back later," Joe said to Sally who also nodded. Sam stood there and watched the two men leave but said nothing at all. Sally looked sadly at him and wondered when his love for Susan had begun.

It was bitterly cold as Joe and Jeff crossed over to the store, and a wind had whipped up making it feel even more frigid. Jeff opened the store and nodded.

"The phone's over there," he said. Joe went to it and picked up but he knew at once that this phone was not working either. He went through the motions all the same just to confirm it.

"Not working; you got another one?" he asked Jeff.

"No," Jeff answered shaking his head, "I only ever needed the one in here." Joe nodded thoughtfully and said,

"Come on over the road and we'll see if I can get the message out from the station."

The phone was dead in the station too. This had come as no surprise to Joe, however; he suspected a downed line somewhere on the mountainside. That was a problem for later. He went to the next room leaving Jeff waiting, to where the radio was located. This was an essential piece of machinery for such an isolated place as Mercy. The phone lines were bound to go down from time to time, and this was a sensible back up for just that occasion.

Joe sat down and set up the machine and was very surprised when nothing but whistling static came to his ears. It was not a particularly bad day for weather and he would have expected a very clear line to Emerson on the radio. He tested it every three days and had never had an issue with it before. It made him feel — as had been the case quite a lot in recent days — very uneasy. Something bigger than he could see was happening around Mercy; he could feel this but had no clear meaning of what that something might be.

'Where the hell are you, Maul,' he thought, 'Is this your doing?'

"We better get out to where Susan was injured," Joe said — purposefully not using the word 'attacked'— coming back to the room where Jeff was waiting.

"No luck?" Jeff asked. Joe shook his head but said no more.

They drove to where Susan's car was abandoned and Joe parked a hundred yards away so as not to disturb the ground in the area any more than it had already been. Jeff opened his door but Joe said,

"No, I'd like you to stay in the car please, Jeff. I want you to just keep an eye out while I'm out there." He nodded to the road as though it were a different planet he was talking about.

"Watch your back, got it," Jeff said lifting his rifle from his lap to show Joe he could be depended on.

The wind wasn't so bad out here on the Emerson back road and it didn't feel so chilly as town did. Joe ambled towards Susan's car scanning the ground and looking all around with each couple of steps. It wasn't long before he was able to see the discoloured ground that Jeff has seen. Even from this distance, he could see it was a lot of blood.

It was whisper quiet as he stood over the bloody mushed snow and the markings on the ground made no sense at all; it was impossible to tell if anything was boot prints, or hoof—prints or anything else.

Looking down the embankment, Joe could see Susan's progress up it to the roadside where Jeff had found her. He looked to the site of the blood in the middle of the road and then down the ditch and saw that it was a very long distance for her to have been thrown. No man could have done that to her; it had to have been some kind of animal. And yet, he thought a blow strong enough to send her so far should have by right killed her or broke her back at least on impact. More information that didn't make sense.

Joe then walked over to Susan's car and looked inside. It was pretty tidy, and he didn't see anything out of the ordinary there. Then going back to the bloodstain he looked to the drag trail that led into the trees. There was no way of telling what animal had laid here, but it had certainly been big; which meant that whatever carried it off must have been big too. The only thing he could think of was a wolf, but it must have been a big one.

Looking back to make sure Jeff was still fine in the car and more importantly was still paying attention, Joe walked to the edge of the road and looked into the trees. Almost at once, a few feet away, he saw the same strange markings that had been at Mouse Allen's place and then patches of white on the barks of some tree trunks caught his eye. It was happening here too; this far out from town. He stepped into the trees and looked for something, anything, that might make even the tiniest thing clearer but again he came up blank.

A stiff breeze rose up and the noise of the groaning creak of the trees startled him. A surge of panic ran though his entire body as this noise suddenly coupled with the feeling that he was being watched — and not by Jeff who wouldn't be able to see him any more since Joe left the roadside. Joe's fright was multiplied when to his horror, he was sure he'd seen the white of the trees spread right before his very eyes, like it had jumped from one tree to another not fifty yards from him.

Pulling his gun, Joe started to back out of the trees the way he'd come in. He didn't have any idea what he thought might be coming for him, but there was no denying the feeling that this is what he thought was happening. It was as if he was being surrounded and cut off and it was a feeling he'd never had before and one he disliked with intense hatred. He slipped a little on the bloodied sludge as he came back onto the road but once he righted himself he hurried back to his car and got in.

"I think we've seen all we're going to see here," he said trying to sound calm.

"You don't look so good, sheriff," Jeff said peering at him with curiosity. "Did you see something in the forest?"

"Nothing I haven't seen before," Joe said and with that he started the jeep, maneuvered it around and drove back to Mercy.

Chapter 17

Sam sat on a chair pulled over to Susan's bedside and he held her hand. Sally had let him come back when his pacing looked like it was going to put a permanent track on her tavern floor. Susan's hand was still as hot as when he had come in, and sweat beads rose continually on her forehead no matter how often he dabbed her with a cool damp cloth. She looked so ill and he was anxious about her. Sam had seen his own grandfather die after an accident when he fell into a fever for three days before finally passing. What he was seeing now was very reminiscent of that bad time. And yet, he knew his grandfather was going to die, everyone there did, but it didn't feel that death was definitely the outcome in Susan's case. Sally had assured him that she was going to be alright, and she had been a nurse. He supposed that qualified her to know more than he did.

Not long after he sat down with her, Susan's breathing became more regular and this had a very calming effect on Sam too. He didn't want to flatter himself that he could have had anything to do with this slight improvement but it made him feel a little better all the same. She seemed more at ease now and looked like she was sleeping comfortably. He looked at her face and thought how beautiful she was, even in this injured and sick state. A flush of embarrassment went through him now at how he had behaved in front of everyone. He'd acted like a teenage boy running around in panic. The shame grew even worse as he thought about the idea that when Susan woke up she would hear all about it too. Even if Sally and Joe didn't rib him about it, Sam was sure that Jeff would tell Mouse and there was no way Mouse Allen was going to keep quiet about a thing like that.

Just then a car door slammed shut and then another and Sam wondered if this was the ambulance arrived. He stood up and kissed Susan's hand before laying it softly back down on her chest.

"I'll be back in a minute," he whispered, "I'm just going to see who that is outside."

On passing through the tavern he saw that Ava and Jarrod were there having something to eat. The smell of the cooking filled Sam's nose, and he felt a pang of hunger in the base of his belly. He went to the door and looked outside and saw that it was not the ambulance but was the sheriff and Jeff getting out of the police car.

Sam walked towards them and noticed that the sheriff looked very pale.

"I thought you might be the ambulance," Sam said when he reached the two men. They looked at one another and then Joe said,

"The phone lines must be down; we couldn't get through to call for the ambulance." This wasn't news Sam had expected; he'd thought the whole time since Joe and Jeff had left that he had been waiting for an ambulance that was on its way from Emerson.

"You tried everywhere?" he asked.

"The store and the station," Joe nodded.

"Maybe my phone is working," Sam said hopefully.

"You can go check if you want, but I don't think it will be," Joe said. "I imagine there's a line down somewhere."

"I'll go check, anyway," Sam said, and he rushed off to his house.

He wasn't too surprised to find that his own phone was dead. It pained him deeply to think that Susan needed medical attention that now was not coming to her. He rushed down the street to Alan's house. He didn't seem to be home, but like all good neighbours in Mercy, he didn't lock his doors. Sam let himself in and looked for the phone. He wasn't sure if there was one here, but he looked in all the places he thought one might be and came up empty.

When he stopped and stood still in the kitchen — the last place he'd looked— Sam suddenly felt very odd. He felt like he had the previous morning in the woods, like there were eyes on him. He tried putting it down to the fact that he was essentially sneaking around someone else's house without permission, but that didn't seem to take with him. He looked through the glass to the rear of the house and it was like he was looking back at something but a something his eyes couldn't register.

Sam swallowed and mustered up the courage to walk to the window and look out more closely. If there was someone out there looking at him he wanted to look back at them and show them that he was not afraid. He knew in his heart that it made no sense that he should have had this feeling of being watched but it felt like such a physical thing he could neither deny nor ignore it.

Out of the corner of his eye, he thought he saw movement, but it was like something imperceptibly slow and he wondered if his eyes were playing tricks on him. It was like something white was spreading from one tree to another about fifty feet away. He looked to the sky to see if cloud formations were causing shadows but all that the sky showed him was one large bank of grey like the entire world was covered by one single huge cloud.

Sam looked back to the trees and then something else caught his eye. The telephone pole closest to the house, and hence closest to the town, had what looked like a creeper of white going up from the ground. The wire was snapped at the top and a thin strand flapped in the wind. The rest must be lying along the ground out there buried in the snow.

This gave him some hope; now that they knew where the fault was it was possible someone in town might be able to fix it. He didn't have those skills himself but Jeff was a mechanic so he might have some knowhow that could be applied.

Another idea came to him just as he was about to leave the house. If the wires were cut off only here at the town, Mouse Allen's house a mile or so down the hill might have a working phone. With this in mind, he ran from the house pulling the door shut behind him. He was making for his own truck when he saw Jeff crossing the road from the tavern to his store. He was still carrying his rifle in one hand.

"Jeff!" Sam called and when Jeff looked up, he said. "The phone line is down out the back of Alan's house!" and then Sam ran on not hearing if Jeff had answered him or not.

All Sam could think about was getting to a working phone and calling for the help Susan needed. He got into his truck, started it and reversed without checking for any hazards around him and then changed to a higher gear too soon to try to get moving faster onto the downhill slope.

In a few minutes he was at Mouse's house and he saw the smashed fence and wondered for a moment what had happened to it. It didn't stay in mind too long however as he rushed for the house shouting out Mouse's name as he ran.

Mouse came out his front door and looked at the approaching Sam with mild curiosity. He waited

"Mouse!" Sam said breathlessly when he saw the big man come out.

"Where's the fire?" Mouse said with a grin.

"Is your phone working?"

"My phone?"

"Yes, Susan is hurt; we need to call an ambulance!" The look of fear on Sam's face and the news of someone hurt took the grin from Mouse's face.

"It's inside, I haven't used it for a few days but I don't see why it wouldn't be working," he said leading the way. In the living room Mouse picked up the phone and put it to his ear and dialled the operator. Nothing. He tried again and the look of surprised confusion on his face was all Sam needed to know that his trip here had been wasted too. He made up his mind in an instant, there was nothing more for it; he was going to have to drive back to get Susan and bring her to the medical centre in Emerson himself, straight away.

"Thanks, Mouse," he said, and he ran out of the house.

"Wait!" Mouse called after him. "What happened to Susan?" Sam was already in his truck by now and his ears heard nothing.

As had been happening frequently for the last while, new ideas kept coming to his head. Sally would not let him take Susan out of the tavern without a fight and it was possible the others would side with her on the matter. But what else could he do? A sickening sense of urgency came over him and he really felt as though he was racing against time. There was only one thing left to do; he was going to have to drive directly to Emerson himself and bring the ambulance back with him. With this in mind, he started the car and turned back heading for the back road to save time. It was all about time to him now.

Not long after getting on to the back road he passed Susan's car, and he looked around at the place where she'd been hurt. He didn't have time to slow down and take a look but he felt sick that she had been alone in this place when she was hurt. He pressed down on the already fully depressed accelerator in anger hoping his own strength might somehow shove the car faster towards his aim.

The truck was moving now at a faster speed than Sam had ever driven it and from time to time on the rises and dips of the road, he could feel he was losing control and the vehicle was floating but each time he got it back without really knowing how he'd done it. Everything was a sign to him now; he was meant to get to Emerson in record time and get the people who would make sure Susan was going to be alright.

The trees on either side of the road were like a blur now and this prevented Sam from seeing what was going on. On either side of him, the trees were turning white faster than he was moving. They came from behind but soon overtook him, like it was some race to a point in the road ahead.

At last, Sam's tunnel vision allowed him to see, and he knew there was something in the road ahead blocking his progress. As he got closer, he saw to his amazement that some of the tree limbs had seemed to come and meet across the road, causing a huge tangle of white limbs directly in his path. When he saw the wood, he knew it was the same as that Maul had shown him and he recalled how brittle and weak it was. He was going to go straight through; the spindly limbs would be no match for the weight and power of his truck. Holding firmly onto the wheel, Sam maintained his course.

The truck slammed into the deep thicket and thousands of snapping noises filled the air, so much so that it painful to hear. Sam screamed at the pain and the realised the truck was slowing down. He couldn't believe it. Pressing hard on the pedal again produced no effect. He could hear the wheels spinning but it didn't feel as though they were on the ground anymore.

Then the truck came to a complete standstill, and the engine gave out in a sputtering groan. Sam sat there looking around in disbelief. The car was at least five feet from the ground and now that the engine had died and there was no more forward momentum. The snapping noises had abated too leaving only perfect snow-dulled silence.

A long gust of exhaled breath escaped Sam's lungs, and he knew for the first time that he had been holding his breath. He didn't believe what his eyes were telling him and he started to have fantasies that he had somehow fallen asleep and left the road and had woken up now in a tree filled ditch. Images of what he'd just seen dispelled this notion, however, and he was left with no choice but to believe that what had happened was real.

There wasn't long to wonder at this however as things got even worse. A new sound rose, one that pinged and crunched like hard snow but in a way Sam's ears didn't recognise. He looked around nervously for the source of the sounds; he couldn't pinpoint it though. It was as if they were coming from everywhere at once. Outside the car he saw that the limbs were moving now, coiling around like snakes and then he knew what was happening!

He scrambled from his seat through the back window and into the bed of the truck. At that moment the squeal of bending metal rose, and the headlamps shattered one at a time like a gun going off; pop-pop. The noise grew louder and more sustained like an orchestra pulling together as different parts of the car body dented and crumpled like paper.

Sam was terrified, and he looked for somewhere to go, but the only option was to jump down to the ground and try to extricate himself from these limbs, which didn't seem like an easy thing to do. There was no other choice though, so this is what he had to do. He leaped from the bed, hoping to clear as many limbs as possible and landed square on his feet and felt pain at the hard slap on the road. His footing went on the ice with his first step and he went down. Though ter-

rified at this it quickly turned to have been a stroke of luck
as he saw some limbs swipe hard at where he had just been
standing. From his position on the ground, an escape route
suddenly became clear, and he dragged himself as fast as he
could through the lower brittle limbs.

The ground was covered in broken pieces of the white
trees and his arms and legs were soon covered in small cuts
and abrasions that stung sharply with each movement of his
body. At last, he was clear, and he pulled away and looked
back into the fold to see his huge metal truck finally collapse
into itself like it had been made of newspaper. The noise was
huge, and it echoed around the forest and mountainside. It
was louder than anything Sam had ever heard in his entire
life.

With that, he turned and ran back towards Mercy. It
would be a very long time before he got back there, but he
knew that was his only chance of survival. Something unre-
al was happening out here — he'd been right about the trees
watching him — and he had to get back and warn the others. Looking back, he was relieved to find that the squirming
mass that had destroyed his truck was not moving and didn't
seem to care that he was getting away — he couldn't believe
he was thinking in this way about trees! But then, all around
him, no matter where he looked he saw the other trees with
their white posts. What need was there to chase him when
no matter where he went on this mountain they would already be there?

Chapter 18

By the time Sam had run out of breath and could only walk, Susan's fever broke as dusk set in. Ava was with her when it happened as she'd offered to help as she waited out her time in Mercy. Jeff hadn't started on their car yet even though he'd brought back the parts this morning. Jarrod had gone over to try to get him to hurry up and she didn't know if he was back in the tavern yet. It was the sudden cooling of Susan's forehead as Ava wiped that was the first indicator she was feeling better.

"Is it safe?" her low voice suddenly asked, urgent and fearful, Susan's eyes shooting open and then darting around the room.

"Oh!" Ava said startled by suddenness. "You're fine. You're in the tavern. Do you want me to get Sally?"

"Is it here?" Susan asked, and she tried to move. The pain shot through her whole body, but it was the sharp one in her ribs that made her cry out. Ava jumped up and held her by the shoulders.

"You've some broken ribs, you need to stay lying down," she said.

"Did you see it?" Susan asked after a few moments of adjusting to the pain.

"See what?" Ava asked. Susan looked at her and then again at her surroundings. This wasn't anywhere she had ever been before, and it certainly wasn't the Emerson back road. Her head cleared as the pain subsided.

"Where am I?" she asked looking at the frightened girl at her bedside

"You're in the tavern," Ava said. "You're safe."

Susan closed her eyes and let her head rest down again on the soft pillow. She was in pain but she was no longer cold and no longer lying on the side of the road; this was all positive stuff.

"How did I get here?" she asked, her eyes still closed enjoying the restful feeling for the first time.

"Mr. Sorkin found you out by your car a couple of miles out of town," Ava said and then after a moments of silence asked, "What happened to you?"

"I found a deer in the road," Susan said but didn't say anymore. Ava looked to see if she had perhaps fallen back to sleep but Susan was not asleep. Images of what had happened were running through her mind. The sounds rushing, snow crunching, the thick smell of blood and the dizziness of being in the air all came together on her and she couldn't piece it all together into one narrative that made sense. Now she was looking face level with the snow and she was scared, something was coming after her, but what? She didn't know. She felt herself on the cold snowy slope of a high hill and didn't know what it meant.

"I'll go get Sally," Ava said worried now in case something was happening with Susan that she did not recognise.

Susan opened her eyes when she heard the door closing and looked around to find that she was alone. Running her hands along her sides, she felt the constant pain held within and a feeling of claustrophobia at the binding of the sheets around her ribs.

The room was nice, however, and Susan began to feel safe. She had survived her ordeal and now there were people around who could help look after her and protect her. The bed felt good under her bruised body and she had to admit she was surprised at how pleasant Sally kept the rooms.

The door opened and Sally popped her smiling head around.

"You're awake!" she said. Susan smiled back and nodded, suddenly feeling like she had been a burden without being aware of it.

"Thanks to you, I hear," she said sheepishly. "I'll get out of here as soon as I can and get home," she added.

"You won't be going anywhere until you're well and rested," Sally said coming into the room fully. "It's nice to have a few people around the place, anyway."

Sally was at the bedside and Susan could see she was giving the patient a once over with her eyes. Susan felt both uncomfortable and grateful at the same time.

"Thanks for fixing me up," she said.

"No problem," Sally said finishing her exam. "The sheriff is outside, and he's hoping to have a word with you?" she said with an eyebrow raised in question. Susan nodded.

"I don't really have too much to tell him, but show him in anyway," Susan said.

"Come on in Joe," Sally called. "She's decent!" she winked at Susan who suddenly looked to make sure that she was in fact decent for a man coming into the room.

When the sheriff entered the room, he looked even more uncomfortable that she felt. Instantly her last conversation with him came back to her mind, and she blushed deeply. A look of concerned sympathy came over his face and he forced a smile her way.

"How you feeling, Susan?" he asked.

"Much better," she answered, though much better than what she wasn't sure.

"Glad to hear it," Joe said nodding his head as though in approval. He let silence fall a moment and then asked, "Do you know what happened to you?"

At this Susan's throat constricted, and the fear came over her once more. Joe looked at her in alarm as she suddenly gulped down breaths and he looked to Sally for a medical explanation.

"It's alright," Sally said going to her and putting her hands on Susan's shoulders. "It's alright."

"Yes," Joe said. "You're out of danger now." Susan, embarrassed, attempted to regain control of her breathing.

"I'm sorry," she said.

"You have nothing to be sorry about," Joe said.

"If you don't feel up to talking now, I'm sure the sheriff could call back later when you're feeling up to it?" Sally suggested, and she looked to Joe. He nodded agreement but Susan could see his reluctance in doing it; she felt there was something he suspected, and the information she had might help him. This is what made her agree to go on now rather than later.

"No, I'm fine," she said. "Just a little wobble." Now it was her turn to force the smile, and it felt even less convincing than Joe's had been.

"Take your time and tell me what happened?" Joe said softly.

Susan lay back in her bed and looked at the ceiling while trying to order her memories in a way that might make sense to someone else.

"I was coming towards town on the old back road," she started. "I came across a stag lying in the road." Joe nodded at this like it confirmed something for him. "I thought it was dead, so I got out and went over to look at it. At first it really did look dead; there were really bad cuts at the top of its hind legs and bits of wood were jutting out it like it had run through a splintered tree or something."

"Wood?" Joe asked, and this surprised Susan. She had expected him to ask why she had gotten out to look at the dead animal but he let this pass without so much as a blink.

"Yes, wood," she answered not sure what else to say about it.

"What did it look like?"

"The wood?"

"Yes."

"Well, I don't know," she said thinking on it. She didn't recall noticing anything unusual about it.

"What colour was it?" Joe prompted, but this only confused her more.

"Colour? Why, wood coloured," she said and then looked to Sally as if she might have the right answer.

"It definitely wasn't white?" Joe asked, and he was looking very seriously into her face. Susan thought back again and now she was not sure at all what colour it had been.

"It could have been," she heard herself say. "But there was so much snow around I suppose everything could have looked white." Joe looked deep in thought on this for a moment and then said,

"What happened next?"

"Well, as I was looking at it, I heard something in the trees..."

"The trees?" Joe asked, and he had an excited look in his eyes and an eagerness in his voice.

"Yes," Susan said and then waited for him to ask more about this but he didn't. "I asked if anyone was there but there was no answer. Next thing I knew something was coming at me and I was running for my life."

"What was it?" Joe asked. "What did it look like?"

"I don't know," she said. "It happened so fast, as first it looked like it was something coming from the bushes at me, but the next second it looked like it was the whole bush that was moving my way."

"Was it a person or an animal?" Sally asked from the doorway. Susan looked to her and shook her head slowly.

"I don't know," she said. "At first I thought it was an animal, but then as I ran I thought — no feel is more close to the truth — feel that it was a person. It felt almost familiar somehow." Joe and Sally exchange glances at this and Susan went red on hearing how this must sound to them.

"You don't know who it was?" Joe asked but something in his question didn't feel true to her.

"If it was a person," she said, "I don't know who it was."

"And then what happened?" Joe asked.

"It hit me from behind, hard, and I went flying into the ditch."

"You were unconscious then?"

"No, not straight away. I was winded and hurt but I was still awake and I could hear it moving around on the road, breathing hard and growling."

"So it was an animal?" Joe asked now. "That sounds like a wolf you're describing."

"It wasn't a wolf," she said dismissively. "We all know what wolves look like around here." Joe nodded in agreement and held his hand up to the ill-advised question.

"Was it still there when you passed out?" he asked.

"I think I heard it dragging the stag away before I went out," she said. "And then, when I woke up I knew I couldn't hear anything for a long time. I knew I wouldn't make it lying in the cold ditch so I did my best to get back up to the roadside."

"You did more than well in that," Joe said with a genuine smile this time. "With your injuries, I doubt many others would have been able to do that."

"She's a tough one," Sally said. "Comes from good stock." Susan smiled at her and nodded thinking of her father.

"That she certainly is," Joe agreed standing up. "I'm glad you're feeling better, Susan. I've been out to the site and so far I can't make sense of it but rest assured I'm working on it and I won't stop until I figure it out."

"Thanks sheriff, I appreciate that," she smiled.

"If you think of anything else, no matter how small, just let me know."

"I will, sheriff, thank you."

Chapter 19

Dusk was rolling over Mercy once more and along with it a growing mist. Joe Moorefield stood at the door of the sheriff's office and looked out into the road. The radio was still down, and this was becoming a major worry to him. Mouse Allen had come into town earlier telling about Sam coming to his house and trying to use the phone and that had put paid to the hopes of communicating with Emerson.

Mouse had also told how Sam had gone off rushing towards the Emerson back road and Joe had an idea he was going to get help in person; the old-fashioned way. Susan seemed to be doing fine, but it wouldn't do any harm to have her looked over by the doctors just in case.

The other side of his brain kicked in then and he wondered about the wisdom of bringing more people here when something very odd was happening. Would he be putting them in danger letting them come for Susan? Perhaps, but from what? That was something he was not able to answer, and it was the crux of everything. What had attacked Susan? What had damaged the young couple's car? Where was Maul? What was this thing growing on the trees? What happened to the phone lines and the radio signal? All these things unanswered in every way. It was not a pleasant feeling.

A pattering noise diverted his thoughts and Joe looked around for the source; thinking perhaps it was dripping from the roof of melting snow. It wasn't all that cold, at least not compared to earlier in the day, but he didn't think it was up to thawing temperature. The noise went on and he cocked his head to try locate it, taking a step out of the shelter of the porch as he did so. Movement in the dark of the road caught his eye and his hand went instinctively to his gun.

Through the thickening mist, he made out the shape of a man moving faster than walking but with a limp that gave him the look of a polio sufferer. It was a gait he didn't recognise and a stranger coming into town on foot made no sense at all. Now he drew his gun and called out,

"Who's there?" The pattering stopped and for a moment silence solidified the air.

"That you sheriff?" the voice of Sam Brainard came back.

"Sam?" The pattering started again as the young man moved closer to emerge from the curtain of mist.

"What happened to you?" Joe asked when he could at last see the dishevelled Sam, covered in cuts and bruising; his clothes torn and his shoes thick with snow.

"It's the trees!" Sam whispered harshly as he fell on Joe and grabbed his shirt front. His eyes darted about in all directions, and what Joe saw in those eyes was akin to madness. He eased his hands onto Sam's wrists and pushed them gently from his clothes.

"Sam?" he said softly. "You're freezing to the touch. I don't think you're well; we need to get you inside and warmed up." Sam stepped back like he'd been shot.

"You have to listen to me," he said. "We're not safe here; we all need to leave, now!"

"Come inside so we can talk about this," Joe said trying to sound friendly and supportive.

"My whole truck was crushed to nothing!" Sam called out plaintively. "Like it was made of paper!"

"What?" Joe said. "Crushed by what? You had an accident?" This would explain the state he was in and also why he was on foot.

"There was no accident," Sam said rushing forward again and speaking in that harsh whisper once more. "The trees closed in over the road and when I tried to go through, they took the truck right off the ground and crushed it!"

Though it was insane to think this might be the truth Joe couldn't help but let his own eyes fall over the trees that surrounded them on all sides. There was something not right about them and he'd known this for days now but surely it was nothing like what Sam was saying; it just wasn't possible. Joe realized that same sense of fear that had overcome him out where Susan Bloom had been attacked was seeping back inside him moment by moment. He played along with Sam to get him inside — or so he told himself he was only playing along.

"We better go inside so we can talk better," he whispered to Sam conspiratorially. Sam nodded and seemed relieved that Joe was listening to him.

"Right," he said, and they drifted inside.

Once in there Joe went straight to the kettle and put it on the boil.

"Get out of those clothes," he said. "You'll get sick. I'll get you something of mine, we're not far off the same size I'd guess," he added looking Sam up and down. "Are you hurt seriously anywhere?" he then asked as he was about to go get the clothes.

"No, I'm fine," Sam answered through chattering teeth. "We need to hurry; is Susan alright?"

"She's much better now," Joe said. "She's woken up and told us she was attacked by a wolf."

"A wolf?" Joe nodded in answer to this. He felt it was better to steer it away from the idea the trees could have been responsible. "She's lucky to be alive then," Sam said. The fact that he thought Susan was better seemed to have a very calming effect on him.

"I'd say she'll be right as rain after a good night's sleep," Joe said to further this calming and then left to get the clothes.

A little while later when Sam was in clean clothes and held a hot coffee mug between his hands Joe decided he'd try finding out what happened again.

"So you say the back road is blocked by trees?" Sam looked up over the rim of the mug and nodded until he swallowed,

"Yes, there's no getting out that way unless you want to get killed." Joe nodded at this.

"I better go out and have a look," he said standing up.

"No!" Sam said grabbing him by the arm.

"It's my job, Sam," Joe said quietly. "Don't worry; I won't try to drive through it. I just need to see what we're talking about."

"To hell with your job," Sam snapped. "You go out there and you'll be killed. I was only lucky to get away!"

"All the same," Joe said pressing on Sam's arm now to get him to let go. "I'll take my chances." Sam let go of him and pushed back into the chair in disgust.

"Go ahead then; go get yourself killed and see how much use you are then to anyone!" Joe felt it best not to say anything else at this juncture and he took his hat and left.

The police jeep was pulling out from the building when Joe had the thought he'd better check the other route to Emerson first, in case Sam was telling some variation of the truth. He set off down the hill to see what he could find out.

Only a mile out on the main road he had to come to a halt, and he looked through the windshield and the most incredible sight yet; even after what he'd seen at the Thorndean place. In the beams from the headlights he marvelled at the white limbs of the trees as they arched up over the road ahead and had then formed an intricate design like a thick web that wouldn't allow anything smaller than a rabbit though. It was both breathtaking and terrifying at the same time. Fear filled his heart and yet he was glued to the seat staring ahead. Whatever this was, it was not good. There was clearly incredible power and — dare he even think it — some kind of beautiful intelligence at play. It made no sense to him in any form.

A shudder from the cold woke him from his trance and Joe backed up with a new sense of respect for Sam for having escaped the clutches of the trees. He turned the jeep and headed back for town. The two roads to Emerson were no longer accessible, and that left only one way out of Mercy. He drove straight through town and up the winding mountain road, past the Thorndean house and up over the crest of the hill. Here, at the highest point he stopped and looked down the steep slope on the other side. As far as he could see in the moonlight the road looked clear, but he didn't feel he could see far enough to be in any was confident it could be an escape route if needed. He set the car in gear and set off intending to go out two miles to make sure.

At first, Joe thought the moving white at the corners of his eyes was just the snow covered ground but when it overtook him in the trees on either side, his stomach tightened up in terror and he slammed hard on the brakes. The jeep slid and tossed all over the road and at one point went up on two wheels against the embankment on the side of the road. The vehicle stopped dead, and the engine cut out. The jeep teetered a moment before crashing back down on its four wheels again.

For an instant all was silent as Joe shook out the dizziness in his head but then a horrible cracking, twisting, grinding noise filled the air, like nothing he'd ever heard before. He covered his ears and saw the trees not twenty feet in front of him bend and expand to form an arch over the road. Then more limbs curled and wisped from the forest and formed the mesh that he'd seen on the Emerson road. The idea that these limbs had the power to crush his jeep as well as him within it filled him with doom.

Then to his surprise, something new caught his eye. In the trees to one side of the road he suddenly saw a twisted and moaning face! He looked in horror as he saw the face, though like that of a man's in many ways, was in fact made of wood and was attached to a large collection of branches and bushes that must have served as the creatures body. It looked as though it was howling or wailing but the noise of the tree limbs was so deafening that Joe could not make it out. Nor did he want to!

He freed his hands to turn the key in the ignition and felt his heart sink even further down into his stomach when the jeep didn't start. He tried again and again and again and at last he felt the vibrations of the engine come to life and the headlights clicked on and Joe caught one last glimpse of the creature before it dashed back into cover and Joe set off at speed back to Mercy.

As he raced back towards town, his eyes frantically looking all around waiting for a ferocious assault from any direction, one thing ran over and over in his mind — Cut off. No matter what he tried to think of only snippets of an idea would come to him before that same phrase — Cut off — would press to the surface again.

The image of what he'd seen flashed before him. What had it been? Was it a man, and if so who was he? Most importantly, what did he have to do with what was going on around Mercy?

It was with great relief that the tiny hamlet that was Mercy appeared once more in his headlights. He didn't let his thoughts dwell on what it was — a relief. This was after all the centre of things, a place surrounded by something sinister and inexplicable. He pulled in at the door to the tavern and got out. He was about to rush inside when he stopped and took a deep breath. He couldn't go in there shouting and frenzied about the trees. They would think he was as crazy as he'd thought Sam was. Besides, he was the sheriff and a certain way of reacting to things was expected of him, of his office.

Looking around the road Joe saw it was deserted. What was the best thing to do? Perhaps it would be best to go back to the station and talk to Sam some more, find out what else he might know, if anything. This idea led him to think that there was possibly a whole lot of information he could gather from almost everyone in town. These things have been going on right under his nose and he hadn't mentioned it to people. It was very possible that everyone had seen or noticed something that they thought was so strange they must have imagined it and told no one else about it.

"A town meeting," he said as the idea struck him.

Joe did his best to compose himself and tidy up how he looked before going into the tavern. He'd seen Mouse Allen's truck, and the out of towner's car outside and he was hoping everyone else in town save Sam would be in there too. He wasn't to be so lucky.

The eyes of Mouse, Jeff and Sally met him as he entered the room and none of them greeted him in any way that he'd come accustomed to.

"I'm calling an emergency town meeting, in here, in half an hour," Joe said.

"Why? What's wrong?" Sally asked.

"What gives, Joe?" Mouse asked at the same time.

"Are the young couple here?" Joe asked ignoring their questions. Sally nodded. "Can you tell them to come too?"

"Of course," she answered. "What is all this Joe?"

"I don't know yet," he said. "But I'm hoping that getting us all together will start giving us some answers."

"Is this about Susan's attacker?" Jeff asked.

"That and a whole lot more," Joe said and then looking to Sally said, "If Susan is up to it, can you get her to come in here too?"

"I'd rather she didn't, but I see this is important," Sally said gravely. Joe nodded and without another word left the tavern to round up the last couple of people in town.

Chapter 20

The room was still and all faces apprehensive when Joe and Sam entered the Lone Wolf Tavern. Ava saw through the sheriff's calm facade and was sure there was great fear in his eyes. She gripped Jarrod's hand tightly and regretted once more ever coming to this terrible little place. The other man, Sam, was covered in cuts and scratches and looked completely worn out.

"What the hell happened to you?" Mouse asked him.

"We'll get to that," Joe said. "First is everyone here?" He looked around the room. Ava looked with him and took in the faces of Mouse, Jeff, Sally, Jarrod and the hunched up Susan in the corner by the fire.

"Alan is not here," Sally said. "I knocked at his house but there was no answer."

"Has anyone seen him?" Joe asked.

"Not today," Jeff said and everyone else shook their heads to agree with this.

"Who saw him last?" Joe asked and Ava saw worry in him.

They looked around at one another before Sally said,

"He was in the night before last."

"Has anyone seen him since then?" Joe asked. No one had. Mouse stood up after a few moments of silence,

"What's this all about Joe, spit it out!"

"Take it easy, Mouse," Joe said, and he sighed glancing sideways at Sam. "Tell 'em what happened to you," he said. Sam looked back at him and then took in the room.

"Joe thought I was crazy when I told him," he started and now it was the sheriff's turn to nod in agreement. "But he's seen the same thing now and knows it's true." Everyone in the room gave Sam their utmost attention and Ava could see that they were all beginning to understand the gravity of something that had taken place.

"I was driving out of town, on the Emerson back road, trying to get to town to get a doctor for Susan," he looked at her at this point and smiled. Susan smiled weakly back to him. "I noticed the whites on the trees, that disease I'd see in a few places around the forest. At first I didn't think anything of it, my mind was too occupied but then more and more trees seemed to be completely covered in it until I realised it was spreading on both sides of the road, and faster than my truck was able to go!"

"Bullshit!" Mouse said.

"What are you talking about?" Jeff asked looking bewildered.

"I've seen this white on the trees," Sally said, "but didn't think much of it. What is it?" her tone was flat and there was no trace of the jovial timbre Ava had come to know in the woman.

"It's something alive," Sam said, "It got ahead of me and then branches closed over the road in front of me and when I tried to go through it with the truck, it caught hold of it and crushed the whole thing like it was a piece of paper!"

At this, everyone in the room save Ava, Joe and Sam talked at once, disclaiming it as rubbish or asking questions that couldn't be made out fully in the noise of joined voices. Finally, Sally rang the old bell that hung behind the bar to get everyone to settle down. Silence fell over the room as everyone looked at her.

"Normally I'd be laughing along with this waiting to see how people were going to react, but I can see in your face Joe that you put some stock in this story."

"I do," Joe said softly. "When Sam came up looking like he did and raving this madness I thought he'd caught some fever from exposure to the cold, but I felt there was something honest in his way and thought it best to go and check."

"What did you see?" Jeff asked.

"I had the idea if Sam was telling the truth the only way out of town was the road over the mountain, so I thought it best to make sure that was clear before checking on Sam's story."

"It wasn't was it?" Ava said, and she knew she was right, she could feel it before he even started to talk about it. Joe looked her in the eyes and shook his head.

"I went out, and I saw what Sam was talking about. The white rushed past me and the road closed over and I couldn't go anywhere. I didn't drive into it so I still have my jeep but there was something else I saw." Joe looked at Susan when he said this last part.

"What?" Susan asked, her lip trembling.

"I saw something, someone, I got the feeling they were behind this and they were who attacked you."

"Who was it?" Susan asked.

"I don't know," Joe said after a slight pause.

"That's not true," Ava blurted, and all eyes fell to her.

"Excuse me?" Joe asked.

"I don't mean about the trees, as crazy as that might sound I believe you, but about you not knowing who it was, I don't believe that."

"Who was it?" Sally asked and Ava felt vindicated that someone else had sensed what she had.

"I don't know what you're..." Joe trailed off as he spoke and a look of surprise came over his face. He looked to Susan again,

"You said you had a sense of something familiar when you were attacked?" he said to her and she nodded. "I felt the same, I didn't understand it at the time but I feel it now, like it was someone not something.

"What are you talking about?" Mouse said, he was clearly very agitated by all that was going on and Ava could see that he didn't know what to believe at all.

"It was Maul, wasn't it?" Sally said.

"I think so," Joe said, "but also not him."

"What the hell do you mean it was him but it wasn't him!" Mouse shouted.

"It was!" Susan exclaimed just then.

"I knew it all along, that man is trouble! His whole bloodline always has been from what I've gathered!" Mouse said.

"This is ridiculous," Jeff said looking at the floor. "I hate Maul as much as the next fella but this is not like him, and it doesn't explain anything about the trees."

"I don't understand what it happening with the trees either," Joe said, "but what I do know is that there is no road out of town, the phones are down and the radio is not working. We're cut off and nobody knows anything about it."

Silence followed this statement and each person let their own thoughts come to them in some effort to understand the situation. Ava couldn't take it anymore and tears streamed down her face. It was the end; if not what else could it be. They had come to this place to die.

"It's alright, baby," Jarrod said taking her in his arms.

"It's not alright," Ava said looking furiously at him, so much so that he was completely taken off guard and took a step back from her. "We're going to die here! Don't you understand that! I told you we shouldn't have come, we should have stayed the night in Emerson."

"No one's going to die," Sally said coming from behind the bar and going to her.

"Sheriff," Mouse intoned, "what are you telling us?" There was fear in his voice that everyone picked up on. All eyes fell to Joe. He looked back at them all one at a time square in the eye.

"I honestly don't know," he said gravely. "But I feel we could all be in danger if we don't stick together."

"Danger from what? I still don't understand what' you're all talking about," Jarrod said. Now it was Ava's turn to grasp his hands in support. Despite her anger at him, she knew he hadn't led them to this disaster willingly.

"I don't hold with any of this bullshit about the trees but if Maul is out there and trying to do harm then I think it's about time we did something about him," Mouse said and then looking to Joe added, "Don't you think so sheriff?"

"I think we should stick together, sit tight for a while. We can try get the phone lines back working and keep trying the radio," Joe answered.

"Sit here and wait to be attacked?" Mouse said with disgust. He took his tankard from the bar and drained what was left in it, wiped his mouth with his sleeve and said, "I'm not doing that. I'm going to go get him before he comes and gets me."

"You go out there on your own and you'll be killed," Sam said.

"I'm not afraid of Maul Thorndean," was the sneered reply.

"You should be," Sally said. "If he is behind this there's no one man in this town who could stand against him and make it out alive."

"I'll change your mind about that quick enough, Sally," Mouse said.

"It's not this Maul person," Ava spoke up. "Didn't you hear what the sheriff and Sam said?"

"All I heard was a lot of things that don't make sense then people saying Maul was responsible for what happened to Susan," Mouse said staring hotly.

"You need to listen to everyone," Jarrod said stepping in front of Ava as though Mouse were about to attack her.

"I'm getting out of here," Mouse said shaking his head in disgust. "You going to try stop me sheriff?"

"I got no grounds to stop you, Mouse, you know that, but I will tell you this. You're not safe out there alone and if

you go I can't say for sure you'll get any help if you need it."
Ava could see the earnestness in the sheriff's eyes and how he
was trying to make Mouse see sense and find his reason but
it was to no avail.

"This town was getting too small for me anyway," he said
as a parting shot. They all watched him go in silence, no one
wasting any more words on trying to change the stubborn
bear's mind.

"What are the rest of us going to do?" Sally asked following a long silence once Mouse was gone.

"I'm going to try the radio again and if that doesn't work
I'm going to see if I can rig something up with the phone
lines."

"I know where the problem is," Sam said. "It's only out
by Alan's house."

"You think you'd be of help with the lines Jeff?" Joe
asked looking at the mechanic cum grocer. He didn't answer
and when Ava looked to Jeff for a reason why, she saw that he
was staring cold and hard at both Jarrod and her. "Jeff?" Joe
said.

"It's them," Jeff said not looking away from the couple.

"What's them?" Joe asked. He looked to Jarrod and Ava
as though for some explanation as to what Jeff was talking
about.

"They brought it here, this thing outside," Jeff said his
voice trembling with anger.

"Don't be so ridiculous," Sally said. Jeff spun to look at
her.

"You explain it then?" he said. "They arrive here in the
dead of night. Their car is mangled — the first thing that's

ever happened like this in this town, and then Susan is attacked and all hell is breaking loose all over the place. It's all since they got to town!" He was pointing at Ava as he spoke and she could feel it so deeply that it could have been the dark barrel of a gun aimed at her waiting to finish her off in judgment.

Everyone in the room was looking at them now and this gave serious credence to what Jeff was saying. There was doubt in all of the eyes levelled their way. They didn't know if it was possible or not, that she and Jarrod had brought this horror down on them.

"We were only passing through," Ava said looking about for someone to believe her.

"You think we can make trees come down and crush cars?" Jarrod shouted and took a few steps towards Jeff before Joe stepped in his path.

"Everyone settle down," he said and Ava felt relief in the look he gave her. He didn't believe this of them. "This has been going on since long before these young people came to town. They are perhaps the unluckiest of us all in that they shouldn't even be here and yet this is happening while they are."

"The simple fact, Jeff, is that we don't have a clue what's going on. It's best we just do as the sheriff says and see if we can contact someone down in Emerson," Sally said. Jeff sat back on his high bar stool and looked at the floor a moment. Then looking to Jarrod and Ava he nodded in what Ava at least thought was his version of an apology.

"I think Sally's right," Ava said and then looking to Jarrod, "Do you think you might be able to do something with the phone wires?"

"Maybe," he said. "I won't know until I can see the problem, but I'm happy to give it a try."

"Good," Joe said.

"I'll take him over to where the fault is," Sam said.

"Wait here until I check the radio at the station first," Joe said. "I want as many people together as we can get for now."

"Then I better go over to the station with you," Jeff said. "We don't want you wandering around on your own either."

"Fair enough," Joe said and the two men left for the station.

"Don't mind Jeff," Sally said when they were gone. "He's just scared and his mouth started running."

"Can happen to anyone," Ava said with a smile of relief. Sally looked at her like a mother to a young child scared of the dark.

"Everything is going to work out fine," Sally said. "You wait and see."

Chapter 21

The only sounds that greeted Mouse Allen on his emergence onto the main road of Mercy was that of creaking trees as they swayed in the breeze. He looked up at them with a mocking sneer on his face but he wished it had been something different he'd heard first and there was no hiding in his heart the plump of fear that had coursed through him on this auditory greeting.

The cold outside and the fear had the effect of calming him down and he had to think for the first time about what his plan might be. Maul was his aim, but no one knew where he was or where he had been hiding for the last few weeks. There was always the Thorndean house, perhaps he'd just hidden from Joe the time he was up there looking. Then there was Susan's attack site, or where Sam said he lost his car, and then finally and what was the most (and very) recent, the road over the mountain out of the town. That's where he'd been this evening.

"I bet you I find you between there and your house, Maul," Mouse said with a grin on settling on this idea. He went to his truck checked his gun and got inside placing the weapon on the seat beside him. Before setting off he dropped the glove-box door and took out his hip flask for a swallow to both warm and rev him up for the task ahead.

His vision was a little groggy as he pulled out from the tavern, but it didn't concern him. He knew the road he was going out on and if everyone was telling the truth, he wasn't going to be meeting any other vehicles out tonight. He rolled over the meandering road, not traveling at his usual speed so that he could keep an eye out to either side in case Maul was on his way into town through the forest close to the road. Another nip from the flask.

The truck slid on the snowy side of the road as Mouse pulled up at the former driveway of the Thorndean place. Checking his gun one more time, he got out and looked around. The night seemed ever colder up here, more snow, more white. He walked a few feet and was suddenly taken aback by the same sight that had assailed Joe Moorefield when he came to look for Maul. Everything was bent and white and leaning to the house like it was dried lava having flowed to it. There was so much white that the light didn't look like night; it was surreal and terrifying and yet strangely beautiful at the same time. There wasn't far Mouse could go before he would have to start climbing over limbs and bent tree trunks.

"You here, Maul!" he called out. "I've come to teach you a lesson once and for all you bastard!" If he was in earshot, Mouse knew that there was no way Maul would be able to hold back at this. He would come crashing from some hiding place and do his best to kill Mouse for talking to him in that way. Silence, however, was all that greeted him. He wasn't here.

"Fuck," Mouse muttered. His hands were shaking, and he knew the initial adrenaline rush was gone now and the next one would not be as strong. If Maul wasn't out where Joe had seen him earlier, Mouse knew it was possible his courage might not hold out for a third look for the man he loathed. He got back in the truck, took another hard swallow from the flask and then sped off towards the crest of the mountain.

It wasn't long before he came across the blockage in the road that Joe had talked about. The car screeched to a halt, a long way from hitting it and Mouse looked in awe and great fear. Even though he'd seen something so inexplicable at Maul's place he still somehow had not believed what Joe or Sam had told everyone. It was just too fantastical to be true.

Now as he was presented with the hard evidence of that same refuted truth he knew that he'd made a terrible mistake in leaving the others. He was not safe here; perhaps not back in Mercy either, but certainly not here. His spine tingled as he felt eyes on him, cold and penetrating like those of a hunter. Hunting him.

With no more thought, he pulled the gearstick into reverse and started to speed backwards to turn the car around. The sound was suddenly like a wakeup call and Mouse Allen looked around in horror as all of the trees, white like never before, seemed to shake into life. The car smashed hard into something and Mouse was jarred so hard he cracked his head on the inside of the windshield. Pain blinded him as he slumped back into the seat and then he felt the oily mess of blood running over his face and the hand that had instinctively gone there to suppress the pain.

With his other hand, he fumbled on the passenger seat for his gun but it was no longer there. Now the panic really set in and he shot out his other hand and searched frantically all over and under the seat. Blood ran into his eyes but he ignored it for now, so desperate was he to be able to defend himself with the comforting weight of steel. He went to one knee and leaning over groped at the floor until at last blessedly he touched the cold of the weapon. He slid his congealing bloody hands around the grip and brought it to his chest and then stopped to listen to the horrifying world around him.

The sounds were of creaking wood and shifting snow. Something was moving around but not in the way of a person or an animal. It was large, lumbering and dragging sounds came from it. Using one of his sleeves, Mouse wiped at his eyes as best he could until he was able to see again. There was a flashing spiralling light in his vision and his head throbbed worse than any pain he ever recalled suffering.

His head spun looking for the source of the sound but everything around him seemed to be moving, every tree, bush and limbs were coiling around the truck. At the sound of the first pop of the metal of the car he knew at once if he didn't get out now he never would. There was no to time to think about what might be out there waiting for him; what waited in the car was the perfect spectre of death.

Mouse kicked the door open and leapt clear of the car. The impact on the ground was hard enough to blur his vision once more, and he lost his footing in the landing and slipped in the snow before falling on his side. He scrambled to his feet and cocked the gun and looked behind at the truck. It was covered in slithering white vines and they closed harder and harder until the pops of metal denting in the car became loud screeching as it was crushed.

Mouse didn't wait to see what the end result would be. He ran as fast as he could into the forest, not thinking at all which way he might be going. All he cared about was getting away from where he was right now. His chest raged with pain as he tried to pull in more and more of the stinging cold air; his heavy body putting a huge strain on his heart as he ran.

"Kill me?" a rasping croaking voice suddenly came from nearby and Mouse stopped dead and spun on his heels almost falling over again.

"Who said that?" he said, not seeing the source of the voice. He knew who it was, was more sure than anything but it had not sounded like Maul — only a little. There was some new quality to the voice like his voice-box had been damaged.

"You better run!" the voice said and Mouse looked to a pile of branches and limbs from where it emitted. As he did, he was shocked to see eyes at the centre of the mess of twigs and white wood. It was hard to comprehend at first, but as the moon shifted from behind a cloud for a moment Mouse could make out the general shape of a man but all around him and even out of his very body grew vines, branches and limbs of the white diseased wood that surrounded the whole of the town of Mercy.

"Maul?" Mouse asked incredulous at what he was seeing. "Is that you?" What answer came from the horror before him was no language Mouse had ever heard. The sentiment was clear, however — anger, fury, rage. It meant to kill him!

Mouse fumbled with his gun and drew it up and fired off two shots in rapid succession as the mass of wood rushed at him. One bullet came home in what would have been the chest were this a man he was facing, but the crack was that of wood splintering and not ribs. The creature grunted and the second bullet seemed to go through the thin twigs on the fringes and off into the distance.

He didn't wait to see how little impact his shooting had made before turning once more and setting off at a run. His thighs ached on the rise and he knew then he was running up hill and that this would be the last mistake he would ever make. Tears streamed down his cheeks at the pounding shuffling sound of the creature coming up behind him. Mouse screamed — there was nothing else he could do. He only hoped that they would hear him back in Mercy and that it might serve as some warning to the others he had foolishly left behind.

Breath was failing Mouse now, and he could feel his body faltering even as his fear urged it on. Two sharp tearing noises disturbed the horrid sounds of the chase and for a moment he didn't know what it was. Then, however, as his feet lifted from the ground and he was no longer going forward, he saw.

Two thick sharpened tree limbs prodded from his chest; the fabric of his shirt dangling from then end of one along with the mixed viscera of what had once been his body. The pain didn't come for another half a second but when it did he had no ability to scream. His body shook with violence on those savage pikes and the white below was peppered with red as the last life drained from the deep rends in his flesh.

In his last moment, Mouse managed to look away from the hellish mush of bloody snow and glancing up the hill all he could see was white; the light of the moon helping make the view perhaps the most beautiful he could ever recall.

Chapter 22

"The sheriff said you should stay here until he gets back," Ava pleaded with Jarrod as he pulled on his gloves.

"It's only across the street," Jarrod said. "You hear what Sam said." Sam nodded and added,

"You can see the house from the tavern door."

"Still," Ava said not knowing what else to say. She looked to Sally for support.

"Joe will only be a couple of minutes, guys, surely you can wait that long?" Sally said to Jarrod and Sam.

"We could," Sam said. "But if the radio isn't working it's best we have that phone line back up and running. Every second could count." Ava could see the wild delirium fear had left him but it was not gone completely. He had the look of a man adrift on a piece of driftwood knowing all the time that at some point the wood would break up in the water. Sally was able to see this too and said no more.

"We can tell the sheriff on our way over," Jarrod said, and he kissed his wife's forehead.

"Be safe," she said.

"Aren't I always?" he answered with a smile.

When the two men stepped outside, they did not go to the sheriff's office to tell him what they were doing but instead went directly across the road to Alan's house.

Sam opened the front door and went inside. Jarrod followed, only mildly surprised that the door was unlocked. Without looking around Sam went out through a back door that this time he had to unlock with a key sitting in place.

"That's the break over there," Sam said pointing. He'd stopped just outside the back door and Jarrod could see the hairs rise on the back of his neck as he looked around at the trees that surrounded the phone pole. Jarrod waited a moment for Sam to walk but it was a long moment and it kept going. Jarrod stepped past him and onto the snow of what served as Alan's backyard, a slope of ten yards and then into the forest.

"Wait," Sam said putting an arm out to block him. "Let me just check my flashlight is working." Removing it from his shirt pocket with trembling hands Sam fiddled with it until a thin, bright beam shot from the glass. He flashed it out towards the trees and they could see within a little better.

Jarrod was stunned by the light as Sam arched it round so it shone in Jarrod's face,

"Listen, I don't know what you believe or don't believe," Sam said, "But you keep an eye on the trees once we go in there and if you see anything moving at all you just run, or if you see or hear me running you just do the same, you got that?" There was such a sternness in his voice that Jarrod nodded in agreement before he knew he was doing it.

They stepped across the lawn, Sam roving the beam in all directions as they went. The only sound was the crumping of the snow beneath their boots.

"The trees are not white here," Sam said stopping once again. Jarrod looked and saw this was true and then looked back to Sam. "This part mightn't be infected yet." Sam said this like it was hard to believe.

"That's good news isn't it?" Jarrod said.

"I suppose it's one reason we are all still alive here, but at the same time it makes me wonder what happened to the phone lines then." The thought came to Jarrod that it was most likely the same person who had screwed up his car, but he felt it better not to bring this up again. Instead, he walked on towards the lines.

The snow was flat and even, no sign of any recent activity but it had been snowing on and off for days now and who knew how long it was taking for tracks to be covered. They arrived beside the pole and looked up and the snapped wire was hanging down about eight feet above them.

"We better find the other part and see what it looks like," Jarrod said looking around at the ground.

"It's been down a while so it's most likely buried over there somewhere," Sam pointed.

The two men separated in a V-shape away from the pole to look for the downed wire. Jarrod leaned over and sifted snow with his hands while Sam used his feet to do the same.

"Any luck over there?" Sam called after about a minute of searching.

"Not..." Jarrod didn't finish what he was about to say. His hand had very nearly come into contact with some snow that didn't look the right colour. "Can you bring that flashlight over here?" he said not looking up but still focusing on the area in front of him.

"What is it?" Sam asked trudging over. The light beam moved and wavered as he walked and once it fell over the marked snow and Jarrod saw the reddish hue he'd feared in the first place.

"I think there's some blood here," he said as Sam came up beside him. He pointed and Sam shone the light on it.

There was no mistaking it.

"That's blood alright," Sam said, his back erect at once and his eyes and the light darting all around them.

"Whose blood?" Jarrod asked.

"Must be Alan's," Sam said after a moments thought.

"You think he's under the snow here?" Jarrod asked. Sam shone the light back on the ground.

"I don't think it's deep enough," Sam answered.

"He could still be alive around here somewhere?" Jarrod suggested. Sam nodded in agreement.

"Alan, you here?" Sam called out. They listened for any kind of response but there was none.

Jarrod was suddenly rigid with fear; up to then he had merely been tense and somewhat amused by all he'd been hearing and seeing. He realised how little stock he'd been putting into what everyone was saying — it was just too fantastical to him. But now he was standing over blood, and what must have been quite a lot before it soaked into the snow and was covered with fresh fall.

"We should go back to the tavern," he said standing up and backing away from the blood. Sam looked at him and nodded but hesitated at the same time. "What is it?" Jarrod asked.

"We should have a look for him," Sam said. "He could be hurt close by and not able to answer us, like Susan had been."

Jarrod felt his common sense pulling him in the direction of the tavern and back to his wife, but his common decency prevailed and he nodded. It was the least they could do for this missing person whom he'd met only two days ago.

"Don't you have a gun?" Jarrod asked. Sam shook his head,

"Not anymore; it got crushed along with my truck." Jarrod had never been a gun owner and most likely wouldn't know what to do with one if he had it, but he never wanted one more in his life than at this moment. His mind went back to how scared Ava had been when she saw something at the window, something he was sure now had been real. If only he'd listened to her, they wouldn't be in this town at all right now.

"Let's look quickly and get back to the tavern," he said.

"I don't like this any more than you do," Sam assured him.

As Jarrod sifted roughly in the snow hoping to find Alan, his mind wandered to the terrifying pandemonium both Sam and Joe had described earlier. It was so unbelievable that at the time Jarrod had not formed any mental picture, but now it was all he could think of. Spindly tree limbs, thin yet strong like spiders legs invaded his mind and fear tickled every part of his body. So afraid now was of he of touching any plant life by accident, he spent as much time looking around him for this danger as he did at the ground for the dreaded shape of death beneath the snow drifts.

"Over here!" Sam voice called, dull and yet somehow reverberating in Jarrod's mind. He looked up and saw that Sam was only fifteen feet away. He was bent over with his light under one arm and both hands sifting snow to either side of a small divot he'd made. Jarrod's feet didn't want to take him over but his sense of duty overrode this feeling. He trudged over, doing his best not to imagine what he was going to see. "He's dead," Sam said standing back up and taking the flashlight in one hand to shine it back down. Jarrod looked through half-closed eyes and he was happy to see that all that was visible was Alan's face. He was stiff and possibly frozen and what blood there was had dried so much that almost all of the visceral power of it had been taken away.

"What will we do with him?" Jarrod asked. Sam shrugged.

"He's probably best off where he is for now; the cold will keep him as well here as anywhere else." Jarrod was happy to hear this but still curiosity got the better of him.

"How do you think he died?" he asked. Sam shook his head,

"I can guess," he said. "But I think the proof of it is buried under the snow. I don't imagine he's in one piece under there." Jarrod regretted asking at once and without warning a spew of vomit erupted from his throat and he was only barely able to direct it away from the body and Sam.

"Sorry," he said wiping his mouth.

"No need to be; this is horrible," Sam said and then turning away said, "Let's get out of here."

"What about the phones?" Jarrod said; he felt a little better having vomited and some of his courage had come back. Sam stopped and looked around for a moment,

"I suppose we should look; that is why we came out here after all."

Speaking nothing more they both went back to searching the snow for the cable. Jarrod's mind was active now with the idea of finding some part of Alan's body, an arm or part of a leg dismembered and bloody in a way his face had not been. He wondered if perhaps there was a hand or some fingers beneath the first slushy blood stain he'd found. He shook his head hoping the thought would be rattled along with it and resumed his scan of the surface.

The clouds shifted once more and Jarrod caught sight of what at first he thought was a thin shadow but when he looked again, he saw that it was a slight ridge in the snow. He moved towards it and as he drew nearer, he became more and more convinced it was the shape and size of the sought after phone line.

His icy hands were numb as he plunged them in and sure enough, under a few inches of covering was the hard cable. He pulled at it looking for the looser end and the sow erupted along the length away from him towards the pole it was still attached to.

"I got it!" he called out, letting it slacken and looking for the other end now. It came free and visible just as Sam arrived beside him. The end was frayed and twisted in every way you can think of. Jarrod looked from it, towards the pole it used to be attached to. He pulled it completely from the snow and walked towards the pole with the line hanging down. He didn't come close.

"Can you fix that?" Sam asked nodding to the mess in Jarrod's hands.

"Not quickly, but there's another problem," he answered.

"What's that?"

"It's not all here; part of it must have been ripped off. This won't reach far enough to connect with the other end, not by a long way."

"This was done purposely," Sam said sourly.

"Just like my car," Jarrod said, "and no tree did that."

"I think we've seen enough here, let's get back to the others," Sam said.

Chapter 23

"Nothing?" Jeff asked as Joe came back from the radio room.

"Same as earlier; I don't know what's wrong with it," Joe said, vexed at not seeing any possible problem he could attempt to remedy.

"What are we going to do?" Jeff asked after a moment of silence between the two.

"Hell if I know," Joe said, and he regretted this honest outlet. "I suppose we get everyone together again, then I'll go with that Jarrod kid to see about getting the phone lines back up." He did his utmost to sound more professional with this last part. Jeff looked outside at the slow falling snow.

"You imagine there'll be any luck there?" he asked.

"I can only hope so," Joe answered.

They were just about to leave the office when suddenly there was a loud crackle of white noise and for a moment what sounded like a warbling distant voice from the radio. Joe and Jeff stared at one another in disbelief and then rushed back inside. Joe sat down at the console and lifted the piece to his ear.

"Hello, is anyone there?" The answer was static but Joe had heard the radio like this before and then suddenly it would come crystal clear in the middle of the message from whoever it might be on the other end. His heart was racing and he couldn't help but feel a smile coming over his face. "This is Joe Moorefield, Sheriff of Mercy, can you read me? Over." The swirling static came back again, but it was diminishing by the second and very quickly it disappeared again. Joe tried again, switching through the channels as he did before but failing just the same. He set it back to the normal channel where the burst had just come from and leaned back in his chair. He thought for a moment and then said,

"We need to be near this radio in case a message comes through," he said. "Can you go back to the tavern and tell everyone to come over here." Jeff looked around a moment and then answered,

"No offense, Joe, but I think everyone would be more comfortable over in the tavern, especially Susan," he said. "We only need one person to man the radio and I can stay here and do that while you go and organise the rest for whatever is coming next."

"I'll come back, or send Sam over in a few minutes so you're not alone for long," Joe said heading for the door.

"Don't worry about me," Jeff said. "Just don't forget to let me know if everyone is skipping town." The smile on his face was forced but even that was welcome to Joe as things stood.

"We won't forget you," he said and then stepped out into the cold evening.

No sooner had he done this though that he found himself suddenly on his guard. He heard the sounds of trudging through the snow and it was coming from across the road. Everyone else was in the tavern so this was unexpected. Joe pulled his gun and peered towards the buildings on the far side trying to pinpoint where the noise was coming from. It sounded like whatever it was making the noise was moving at a lope or jog and yet it didn't have the rhythm of either beast or man that he knew.

When he localised the sound at the front of Alan's house, Joe aimed his gun towards the front door. There was a moment of joy when he thought perhaps it was Alan himself coming out from wherever he'd been but he wanted to be sure before calling out. Then he saw that there was more than one shape moving at that doorway and this didn't make any sense to him at all. He cocked the gun and gripped it more firmly.

"Who's there?" he said wishing instantly he'd gotten Jeff to come out with his gun too but not wanting to call for him now and show any weakness to whoever was over there.

"Take it easy, Joe," the voice of Sam Brainard came back.

"Who's that with you?"

"It's me, Sheriff, Jarrod," a nervous voice called out.

"What in the hell are you two doing over there; I told you to stay in the tavern," Joe asked vexed.

"We know, but we wanted to see if we could get the phone lines back up quickly," Sam said.

"Did you?" Joe asked, no longer caring so much that they hadn't listened to him.

"No luck; they're beyond repair," Sam said walking out of the shade of the house with Jarrod close on his heels.

"That's a pity," Joe said shaking his head. "Jeff is inside at the radio but it's not working yet either."

Sam and Jarrod were looking at one another now in a way that told Joe something else was up. He looked to Sam, knowing him the better with a raised eyebrow. "What is it?"

"We found Alan," Sam said. "He's dead."

"How?" Joe asked.

"We're not sure; he's mostly buried and frozen in the snow but there's blood about the place so it wasn't a heart attack." The cynicism in Sam's voice surprised Joe for a moment but then he recalled what kind of day the man had been through and it didn't seem so odd. There were many more questions Joe could ask about how long they thought the body was there, what wounds could he have based on the amount of blood, but he knew these were pointless. They would only be answered when he went to see for himself.

"Let's just get everyone back inside the tavern," he said as he walked that way. Joe knew they would look at one other, perhaps confused by his not going directly to see the body but everything was different now. Under normal circumstances — if there was such a thing where a dead body was concerned — Joe would have gone straight to the scene to make sure it was closed off and any evidence could be preserved. That wasn't going to make any difference tonight; he could feel that in his bones. It was possible he would find something out at the scene, but considering what he'd seen and heard so far it didn't seem likely. What needed to happen was for everyone to try to get out of town. As the certainty of this came to him, he wondered why he hadn't already tried to do this. What would sitting in Mercy waiting for an attack succeed in doing for anyone?

"You don't want to go to Alan's body?" Jarrod asked timidly.

"It won't do any good," Joe said turning to the two men. "We all know what's going on here is impossible to understand. We need to try to get out of town, all of us."

"How?" Sam asked.

"On foot is the only way, down through the hills," Joe said.

"On foot!" Jarrod cried.

"What makes you think walking through the trees is going to be any different to trying to leave by the road?"

Joe didn't have any answer to this but even if he had, he never had time to give it. Gunshots echoed from far off over the crest of the mountain. The three men looked at one another and Joe fumbled through his pockets for his car keys.

"That's Mouse," he said. "Go inside and get Jeff and then go to the tavern and get everyone ready to leave when I get back." Joe stopped a moment and then went on, "If I'm not back in forty-five minutes get started without me. I'll follow on."

"Where do you expect us to go?" Sam asked.

"Pass by the old mine shaft and then down through the old miners huts and keep going as far as you can. I'll find you."

"Where are you going?" Jarrod asked.

"I've got to go and see what trouble Mouse has found for himself."

"Why don't I come with you?" Sam offered but Joe shook his head at this idea.

"I want as many of you together as possible," he said.

He left the men standing there and got into his jeep and sped off up the mountain. He guessed Mouse had gone to where Joe had seen the trees close off the road earlier in search of what he thought was Maul. Though he thought the worst about what might be going on there, Joe guiltily found himself hoping that perhaps it had been Maul all along and that Mouse had managed to put an end to it once and for all.

At the top of the mountain, Joe got a brief glimpse of the land below to the south and to his astonishment it looked like the larger town of Centrepoint, some twenty miles away, was completely ablaze.

"What in hell is going on in the world tonight?" he asked aloud. It looked like the whole town was alight. The smoke was thick in the air like storm clouds even from this distance away. The view was fleeting however, and the jeep dropped down the other side and below the tree line once more.

Joe could see what turned out to be the crushed husk of Mouse Allen's truck for a long time before he knew what it was. A black misshapen lump in the centre of the road presented in his view for a full minute before he was close enough to make out anything that resembled a vehicle part. Had Mouse been firing his gun from within the truck or outside Joe thought as he pulled to a halt, his jeep lights beaming on the mangled corpse of the truck.

It was an incredible sight to see the vehicle so completely demolished and this was the first time he understood how lucky Sam had been to escape. He also had some idea now of what he'd escaped himself. It was too hard not to ask himself what he thought he was doing driving back out here after what happened earlier.

Joe pushed himself from the car before his courage failed him. Whatever else was going on it was still his duty to see what had happened to Mouse and try to save him if he could. His gun was in his hand before he knew he'd drawn it and the spindling fear and sense that he was being watched returned like nausea to his stomach. Walking to the shell of the truck, he decided against calling out to Mouse. He kept his eyes on the trees on either side of the road waiting for any movement to set himself to running back to the jeep.

He felt the crunch of broken glass beneath his boots just before the loud crack of a larger shard punctured the surrounding silence. His eyes darted around waiting for his noise to be the signal for all hell to break loose. The moment of terror ran longer than expected and it was clear nothing had occurred as a result of the sound. The trees, limbs and snow all around looked no different or disturbed that it had a few moments ago. A voice in his head was saying, 'Just go back; get out of here. What good do you think you can do?' but to his credit Joe did his best to drown it out.

On the ground he saw streaks of blood near a mound of snow and then saw the traces of what must have been Mouse's escape from the site. Footprints and bloodstains punctured the snow. Thank God he wasn't still in the vehicle when it was crushed. Joe began to walk in the direction of the trail but it wasn't long before his joy at the idea of Mouse escaping turned to horror as he saw the slumped shapes that were once the big man's body lying in a sea of blood beneath some trees.

Joe stopped moving, terrified and aghast at what he saw. He was not close enough to see clearly (and didn't intend on getting there) but he was sure Mouse Allen had been torn in two and that could only be done by the same power that crushed the truck. He looked at the trees that over hung the body knowing they had been what killed Mouse but yet not seeing any trace of blood on the limbs. It didn't make sense, but then what did right now.

Sense now would be to do everything he could to get out of Mercy and down off this mountain. Once more the idea of leaving alone and just making it out pressed him but he walked back to the jeep and drove back to Mercy to do what he could to get everyone out of here and hopefully to safety.

Chapter 24

The tavern was buzzing with raised voices, speculation and arguments that all fell silent when the sheriff entered.

"Where is he?" Jeff asked with a look of grim acceptance already on his face.

"Mouse is dead," Joe said. "Near where I had my incident earlier this evening."

"Two dead and one person lucky to be alive!" Jeff called out pointing to Susan. "We've all sat around long enough; we need to get out of here!" Voices erupted with opinions once more and Sally had to ring the shrill bell to get everyone's attention again.

"Let the sheriff talk," she said looking to Joe. "How was Mouse killed?" she asked more quietly.

"I can't be sure, but it looks like the trees had something to do with it." Even after all he'd seen he still found it impossible to believe he was saying this. "No man could have done what I saw, and his truck is crushed to a cube too."

"So what are we going to do?" Ava's timid voice asked through the silence that followed what the sheriff had told them.

"Jeff is right," Joe said. "We need to get out of here right now. All the way here I was looking at the trees and I can only draw once conclusion from what I saw. Whatever is happening with the trees, they are all dying and that whiteness on them is getting closer to town by the minute."

"You expect us to get out of here on foot?" Sally asked and Joe nodded.

"I don't see any other way," he said. "We know what happened to those who tried to leave by the roads."

"What about Susan?" Sally asked. "She's still recovering."

"I'll be fine," Susan said with an obviously forced upbeat smile on her face.

"There won't be any recovering going on here when the trees close in on the town," Jeff said looking sharply at Sally.

"Don't even think about getting on my case, Jeff," she replied hotly. They looked at one another a few moments more and then Jeff looked back to Joe.

"I say we have ten minutes gathering what we need and then we go. Anyone not back here by then we leave without them!"

"Take it easy, Jeff," Joe said. "We're not leaving anyone behind."

The room fell silent again, and they all looked around at one another. Fear was painted on every face in the room. The feeling that none of them was going to make it out of here alive was powerful but no one gave voice to it. Each one thought of the hardship of traveling to Emerson cross-country in the current snowy, cold conditions. If that wasn't tough enough on its own, there was also the chance that any tree they passed along the way could grab hold of them and kill them at any moment.

"Come on, everyone," Jarrod said taking Ava by the hand. "We can do this; we can get out of here."

His attempt to rally fell flat, only Ava even acknowledged him with a thin smile.

"Sally can you rustle up some flasks of coffee and some food to bring with us — we shouldn't need much?" Joe said. The tavern-keeper nodded.

"Jeff and Sam, go to your store and house together and get any guns and ammunition you have and some warm clothes. Stay together," he stressed.

"What are you going to do?" Sally asked.

"One more check on the radio and then getting my own ammunition and spare guns," Joe answered.

"Should I go with you then?" Jarrod asked. Joe looked at the scared young man and was about to shake his head but thought better of it.

"Yes, I should heed some of my own advice shouldn't I?" he smiled at Jarrod and winked at both he and Ava. Jarrod smiled back and Joe felt that smile showed the boost in confidence Joe had intended had been received. "Will you three ladies be alright here for a few minutes?"

"Go, we'll be fine," Sally said speaking for them all. Joe nodded and then looked at the men ready to leave.

"As quick as we can," he said. "Don't try anything alone, if you even think you see something call out for help, got it?" The men all nodded. "Let's go, then."

WHEN THEY HAD LEFT, Sally looked at the two younger women and said,

"How are you feeling?" to Susan.

"I'm still in a lot of pain," Susan answered, tears that she'd been hiding up to now coming to her eyes. "I don't know how I'm going to make it down the mountain." This last word broke, and she bent forward crying into her hands. Ava was close to her and put an arm around her and Sally came over and added hers to the circle.

"Don't you worry," Sally said. "Those hiking trails are not so bad. I don't suppose you'll be happy while we're moving but once we get to Emerson, we can get you straight to some real medical help."

"They'll fix you up good and proper," Ava added.

"I'm sorry," Susan said. "I shouldn't be thinking about this right now with everything else that's going on around here."

"You being hurt is a huge part of what is going on around here," Sally reminded her. "You survived that attack; you're tougher than you think."

"Emerson is not all that far, anyway," Ava added, hoping to sound cheerful.

Sally broke from the hug with a parting squeeze on both of the other women's arms.

"We better get set," she said walking over to start preparations on the flasks and rummaging up some light food for the hike.

"Do you have clothes that will suit walking in the snow?" Susan asked looking at what Ava was wearing.

"I don't think so," she answered, thinking about this for the first time. They were only supposed to stop off in this place for a bed for the night on their way West and hadn't packed too much at all.

"We'll have to get to mine for some clothes then, you're not far off my size so we'll be fine," Susan smiled through her pain.

"I guess the sheriff wasn't thinking of the women when he set off," Ava smiled back.

"I guess not."

"GOD DAMN IT!" JOE CALLED out in frustration when the radio once more gave no sign of life in response to his switch tripping and turning. It was not that he expected it to work this time; it was just that it was his last hope of getting help to come to them before making this trip down the mountainside. He knew that Susan was not going be able to make any kind of progress at all and they were going to have to practically carry her all the way, but what could he do about that?

"How long do you think it will take to get down to Emerson?" Jarrod asked when Joe came back to the office where he was waiting.

"I don't know, but it will be by light tomorrow I imagine." Joe moved around the rooms collecting clothes and the small tool belt he usually had when he went for a long hike.

"Do you know how to use a gun?" he asked Jarrod. Jarrod looked at the pistol in Joe's hand and nodded slowly,

"Yes, but only a rifle," he said.

"Well, this is easier," Joe said thrusting the gun into Jarrod's hand. "Safety here, hold with two hands, point and shoot, that's it. The recoil might be stronger than you expect so just watch out for that and don't point it unless you aim to fire it."

Jarrod nodded as the instructions were recited and he let Joe move his arms and hands to mimic what he was instructing.

"Got it," he said when the ten second long shooting class was over.

"Put this on over those clothes," Joe said handing Jarrod some warm clothes and gun belt.

Jarrod got into the clothes as Joe got himself sorted for ammunition and supplies.

"Do you think the guns will be of any use against this thing?" he asked after a long silence.

"I have no idea," Joe answered. "But I know I'd rather have the guns than not." Jarrod nodded; he felt the same way. Deep down he still felt that this had to be the work of a person; and he knew that guns definitely worked against those.

"WHERE ARE YOU GOING?" Jeff asked when Sam walked up the middle of the road. They had collected clothes, weapons and tools from their homes and were on the way back to the tavern — or so Jeff thought.

"We need to get clothes for Susan," Sam said, "and I imagine there will be at least one more gun there too."

"Sally will have clothes for Susan," Jeff said but even as he was talking he followed Sam. You couldn't have too many guns in a situation like this.

"Clothes that fit," Sam said.

"Fine," Jeff said coming up beside him. "But we need to be quick."

They entered the house, and both men looked around. It was odd how even in such a small community as this the locals had never really been in one another's houses. The tavern was the usual congregational place and everyone home was mostly private to themselves.

Sam could smell Susan in there and his heart panged at the thought of what might have been.

"You look for the guns and I'll get some clothes," he said. Jeff nodded and went about his task. Sam walked to the doors that were closed off the hall and opened the first one. It was a bedroom but not the one he was looking for. This must have been where Susan's father had slept and by the looks of it, the room had been left as had been while he was alive. It was clear that Susan even kept the place spotless with not a sign of dust on any surface.

The next door was Susan's room. He stood in the doorway a moment and wondered at it. There was nothing particularly special about it and she didn't even seem to have anything particularly feminine about the decor. Her smell was strongest here, however, and it overpowered him. He felt tears sting his eyes and his fists clenched in anger at the unjustness of what was happening. He didn't know if they were going to make it off this mountain but he vowed to Susan in her own bedroom that he would do all he could to make sure they did.

"Hurry up in there!" Jeff's voice called out. "I've got a hunting rifle and a box of shells here." Sam could hear the rattle of the shells in the box as Jeff shook them.

"Coming now," Sam said, and he bent quickly to the chest of drawers by the bed and pulled out some clothes he thought would be warm. He pooled up a big armful, not wanting her to feel like he'd chosen the wrong things for her. As he stood up, he saw a framed photograph on the nightstand. It was Susan with her father and she was old enough that he thought this was probably the last photograph ever taken of them together. He made space between two fingers and picked it up; he was sure she would want this if they got out of here in one piece. He could imagine her beautiful smile after they were safe and he handed it to her. It was a moment he longed to become a reality.

EVERYONE WAS BACK IN the Lone Wolf Tavern and they looked at the assortment of clothes and supplies laid out on the tables.

"We need to get moving fast, so everyone who isn't already dressed to go, do so now while we pack up this stuff," Joe said. He could feel his heart racing like he was back in high school just before a big track meet where his father would have expected him to win.

"So what's the plan, Sheriff?" Jeff asked as they packed.

"We'll use the easy path to the mine opening and start across towards the lake and then down from there. Considering the conditions I think that'll be the best route, but I'm fresh here," he smiled. "So if any of you locals know a quicker way that will be passable I'm all ears?" Joe could see that both

Sam and Jeff were thinking on this, hoping to find a better route but he didn't think they would.

"Sounds about right," Jeff conceded.

"We stay together and everyone who can use a gun should have one," Joe went on.

"What if we get separated?" Ava asked.

"We shouldn't, but if somehow we do just follow any trail that goes downhill; that's about the best I can say." Joe walked over to Susan. "I know you're still in a lot of pain and I'm not going to tell you this run down the mountain is going to be pleasant for you, but we will be there to help all the way; you just have to do your best to keep moving, alright?" Susan nodded,

"I'll get there," she said, and she looked to Sally and Ava and smiled.

"Right!" Joe said addressing the room again. "We need to leave now. We have no idea what we are up against but we all need to keep our eyes open. If we are attacked, shoot if you can but not if you think it will endanger any one of us."

"Shoot at what?" Sam said though it seemed like he let it slip by accident.

"We can only hope that lady luck is on our side tonight," Joe said and with that, he started for the door.

Chapter 25

By the time they reached the old mine entrance it was clear how hard a night was before them. Susan was in agony with every step and any attempt to half carry or aid her seemed to end in even worse pain for her. The trip to this point had taken an hour which was almost triple the time it took on a normal day.

"You need to go on without me," Susan said as she drew breath.

"That's not going to happen," Joe answered her. Sally looked down at their tiny town and it struck her eye how black the trees looked around it.

She cast her eyes up the mountain and saw where the white took over and covered the higher slopes and then she looked down the mountain and saw pockets of white spread out all over. She didn't know the route Joe had proposed, but she thought it best to point this out to him lest they come through one of those white areas unprepared. She took him to one side, but Jeff saw and walked over.

"This is no time for secret conversations," he said. He looked not only angry but almost betrayed.

"I haven't even said anything yet," Sally snapped back. "It was going to be general knowledge in a second, anyway."

"Then why tell him first?" Jeff nodded to the sheriff as he said this. Sally didn't have an answer for this and for the first time in a long time she was stumped.

"I guess there's no reason," she agreed.

Everyone else was aware of the little spat now and all eyes were on Sally when she turned to face the group.

"If you look up and down the mountain from here," she said waving her arms in both directions at once. "You will see that the white stuff is all over the higher slopes but it's spread about down below." They all looked and each of them noted that it was true. "I just wanted to make sure none of those white areas on the way down were part of the route Joe had proposed.

"Are they?" Jarrod asked looking to Joe. Joe didn't answer for a moment but took in the full vista available to him and then sighed.

"Some of them are on the route I had in mind," he said. "But it's worse than that."

"How so?"

"Those white spots cover all of the routes down that I know of," Joe said. He beckoned Jeff and Sam over. "Do you know of a way down that avoids all the white parts?"

Sam and Jeff looked, each man scanning different parts of the forest before slowly turning to look at one another and then to Joe shaking their heads.

"It's like it knows the place!" Sam said.

"There's only one person who knows the whole mountain and could block off strategic points like that Sheriff, and you know who I'm talking about."

Joe nodded but still didn't want to think it could be the case.

"Maul," he said.

"You guys are going potty if you think Maul can control the trees!" Sally said.

"This whole situation is insane," Jeff said. "Maul being behind it is not stranger an idea to me than what has already happened.

"You think it was him, don't you Susan?" Sam asked. Everyone looked to the wounded woman leaning against a tree. Mists of uneven exhalations floated from her mouth before she spoke.

"I wasn't sure," she said. "But I think it was him, only not in a form any of us would ever fully recognise him."

"What the hell does that mean?" Jeff exclaimed.

"He's changed," Susan answered in her still in pain measured tone. She was looking off into the trees. "Something happened to him too, I think something changed him."

"Changed him to what?" Ava asked.

"Something like the trees, whatever evil it is within the trees."

No one spoke as they thought on this. It made no more real sense to those who knew Maul than to the young couple who had never lain eyes on him.

"So what do we do?" Sally asked looking to Joe. He looked slightly frazzled, more so than he'd been so far and Sally felt a little sorry for asking. He was the leader because of his job but she was sure no member of the police force had ever been asked to deal with something like this before.

"I suppose we head down as far as we can and then do our best to avoid the white sections." No one came up with a better idea so they set off soberly once more.

The mood changed with each step in the snow. At first, they had been cheerful if a little nervous at the thought of getting out of here but now there was only misery and dejection evident in the group. No one spoke, each one of them running their own thoughts in a seemingly hopeless attempt to understand anything that was happening.

Sally looked around at the group as she walked along with Susan. She'd never seen so many of the locals in one place that was not her tavern room. They all looked so odd and out of place, like they were not the people she knew at all, or that she had never actually known them properly in the first place.

Joe had always taken care of anything that happened with an even hand and cool temper, but even he was now showing signs of strain that she wouldn't have expected of him. Jeff was not far off his usual cantankerous self, but without Mouse he seemed less somehow, like part of him was missing.

As she thought about her observations of the others, her mind drifted to what they might think of her. It was true that she too must seem different today than any of them had ever known her. Truth be told she was scared — and not just a little. This was a very odd sensation for her and not one she'd grown up being used to. Her father had raised her to be fearless and more man than the men around her but she didn't feel this right now. All she wanted was to be gone from this place despite how much she had loved living here.

So lost in her own thought was she that she bumped into Jeff's back before noticing that everyone else had stopped. Looking at them, she saw they all head their ears cocked. They must have heard something that she missed. She wanted to ask what it was, but she knew by the tense pose of each of them that silence was required.

As she watched, she saw Sam pointing into the trees and the other following his direction. Then Sally heard it too; a noise like thin twigs scraping on a windowpane in the breeze. It was getting louder but still didn't seem to be close. They all got their guns ready, Sally letting go of Susan a moment to set her own rifle towards the noise.

"Call when you see something?" Joe said.

The whole lot of them looked into the darkness between the trees and listened as the sound grew louder and then seemed to be suddenly be approaching much faster than before.

"It's coming!" Jeff shouted, and he took a step forward to plant his feet against the shooting he was poised to do once anything came into sight.

"Don't shoot unless there is something to shoot at!" Joe warned.

The noise was loud enough now that Sally barely heard what he said. A quick glance at the young couple showed Jarrod holding a pistol in two shaking hands and Ava trembling in terror just behind him. She too held a gun, but it was not raised to fire. It wasn't something that was in her.

Sally looked back to the trees just in time to see what looked like hundreds of tendrils spring forth as though from nowhere and dart between each of the group. Gunshots rang out, and bright lights flashed and Sally shot her own gun at the mass of limbs coming at them. The screams and shouts of all of them filled the air and then she saw people being knocked over or sent flying through the air. She heard Jarrod cry out in pain and as she looked at him saw a huge gash opened up on his chest, blood spreading quickly to his shirt. Ava screamed and grabbed hold of him but at that same moment she was sent flying by a limb and her grip on his arm sent Jarrod stumbling over onto the ground.

Sally fired again and again at the some of the larger limbs and she saw them shatter and splinter to in the air, dust flying from the dry interior like chalk in the moonlight. She was getting ready to fire again when she suddenly felt a huge pressure around her waist and she was lifted from the ground. It took her so by surprise that she dropped her rifle and pulled at the branch before she even saw it. She kicked wildly with her legs and pulled her torso this way and that in an effort to wriggle free but the powerful supple wood held tight without lessening its grip.

"Joe!" she shouted seeing that he was still on his feet and shooting, but as he looked at her he too was swiped hard across the chest and sent tumbling backwards losing hold of his gun as he fell. She pulled and punched at the coiling wood and then it began to constrict and the pain in her midriff just above her hips was searing. She cried out in pain.

"No!" a new and gruff voice shouted out above the din. The deep voice had come from within the trees and then something new and bulkier came crashing through the limbs at an angle that cut them off from the falling group. No one was firing anymore and the new visage pounding from the forest like a wild animal took all their attention.

Limbs and branches snapped and pulverized to dust and it moved through the melee. It was like a man but seemed to carry behind it a huge bush of tree limbs and twigs that was snapping and cracking just as the limbs it forced its way through. Squealing sounds like a wounded animal came from all around as the limbs pulled back like fingers burnt in a fire. The shape moved through to where Sally was and smashed through the large branch that held her. It broke clean in two and Sally fell the few feet to the ground and rolled over backwards. Without a moments pause the beast moved off at great speed in the direction the attack of the trees has come from. It wailed and roared in a way that sounded almost human and soon it was gone deep inside the forest and they could hear neither it nor the scuttling of wood any longer.

"What the hell was that?" Jeff said getting to his feet.

"Whatever it was it just saved our asses!" Sam said. He too was standing up again though it was taking some effort and Sally saw that many of his wounds from earlier were bleeding again.

"It was Maul," Sally said.

Those back on their feet looked at her.

"You saw him?" Joe asked. Sally shook her head,

"No, but I know it was him. He wanted to save me."

"Jarrod!" a shrill scream came from behind them. They all turned to see Ava kneeling over her husband. Everyone rushed over and Joe bent down to him.

"Sally, can you have a look at this," he said. She bent down and looked at Jarrod's chest and then to his face. He was conscious but looked very pale and ready to pass out.

"How does it feel Jarrod?" she asked trying to gain eye contact with him.

"It hurts," he managed to say, a massive understatement Sally thought but at least he was talking.

"I'm going to give this a little clean to make sure it doesn't get infected," she said, "It's going to hurt but I have to do it." Jarrod nodded and then looked to Ava with a thin blue lipped smile.

"You probably won't want to see this," he said.

"I'm staying right here," Ava replied squeezing his hand.

As Sally cleaned and dressed as best she could Jarrod's wounds, the rest of them talked about what had just happened.

"Our guns are useless against it!" Jeff said and there was a huge surge of anger in his voice.

"There's no argument there," Joe said. "But we need to think of a way to deal with it."

"I think we'll need to split up," Sam said. The others looked at him. "We can't take it on so we need to try to run from it. That's how I survived earlier, and you too sheriff." Joe thought about this for a moment.

"We need to get Jarrod and Susan back to the Tavern," Sally said. "They won't be able to make it out like this."

"We can't go back now!" Jeff said he looked to Joe for agreement on this. Joe looked in Sally's eyes and said,

"We have to get the wounded back to somewhere we can take care of them."

"This is fucking ridiculous!" Jeff cried. "What the hell did we risk our lives coming this far for?"

"We tried, and it didn't work," Joe said, "We can't try the same thing again; we need to learn from every mistake we make!"

"I've learned from my mistakes already," Jeff said, "I've learned not to let any of you people talk me into anything else. I'm going down the mountain. Alone if I have to, but anyone who wants to come is welcome."

Jeff looked around by no one was in agreement with him.

"Come back to town with us," Sally said looking at him. Jeff looked back bitterly and then sighed.

"I don't wish any of you ill but going back there is a death sentence, I can feel it in my bones," Jeff said pleasingly. "I've got to go with what I think is right and that's getting out of here."

"We can't change your mind?" Joe asked. Jeff shook his head. "Well then we wish you the best, Jeff," Joe said holding out his hand. Jeff shook it.

"If I get out, I'll get help to you somehow," Jeff said with tears forming in his eyes.

"Let us know you're off the mountain with three bursts of your gun, will you?" Joe asked.

"I will."

"You don't want to be out there on your own," Sam said. "Take it from someone who knows." Jeff smiled at him.

"I appreciate the concern son, but my mind is made up."

Jeff took up his pack and checked his gun. He nodded to the group. "I hope to see you all again soon; best of luck to you." He walked away with murmured goodbyes from the group behind him, each one of them assuming they would never see him again.

Chapter 26

The slog back towards Mercy was even more miserable than leaving. Each of them was hurt — mostly cuts and bruises save Jarrod, and they had been severely demoralised with the ineffectiveness of their weapons. Susan was having a lot of trouble breathing and Joe felt that it wouldn't be long before fever was back upon her. Sam was practically carrying her now despite his own worsened injuries. The whole lot of them looked like soldiers after battle more so than ordinal people living in a mountain idyll.

They stopped as before by the old mine entrance and looked over the mountain. Joe had been taking much of the weight of Jarrod and he was exhausted. The cold air felt good in his lungs as he breathed more easily without that strain.

"This all looks different to earlier," Sally said. Joe looked and saw that she was right. The white from the top of the mountain had spread like a blanket even further down towards Mercy than before and below them the patches of white were not only joining up now but were also coming closer to the town. They were being surrounded and hemmed in and there was nothing they could do about it.

"We better keep on moving," he said, not wanting anyone else to start dwelling on the negative thoughts trying to invade his own mind. Jarrod moaned at the judder of his body as they moved again.

"Stop it, you're hurting him!" Ava cried out pulling at Joe's arm.

"We have to keep moving," he said to her. "It won't do him any good to stay out in this cold in the shape he's in." Ava looked to her husband with fresh tears in her eyes and nodded.

"Can you make it just a little farther?" she asked him. Jarrod did his best to smile and after drawing breath managed to say,

"You're the one holding us up." Ava smiled back at him and squeezed his hand a little and then looking at Joe said,

"Take it as easy as you can, sheriff."

"I will," Joe said glad that the delay was over. He looked down over the hills below and wondered how, if he was still alive, Jeff was getting on. Then setting a firm foot to the ground he pressed forward with Jarrod's weight on his body.

They were moving now and Joe leaned forward a bit to take some more of the load on his back when suddenly he felt the full presence of the young man disappear from his back. He heard screaming but the disappearance of the weight so sudden and his leaning forward sent Joe tumbling down a few feet before he could halt his progress and look around to see what was happening.

Everyone was standing aghast and looking at the sight of Jarrod being pulled along the ground by a cluster of long wiry tendrils that had shot out from the woods without sound or warning. Jarrod was crying out in both pain and fear and Ava scampered after him and grabbed hold of his hands. It was no use and the small girl was no match at all for the power of the trees and she fell to her knees and was dragged along too.

Joe got his feet and pulled his gun and fired a few shots beyond Jarrod at the tangle of knotted tendrils where they joined up but his bullets only shattered small pieces and not stopping them in the least. Then to his horror the blood started to flow.

Jarrod's sides were opening up with the pulling and twisting and thick gobbets of blood oozed out and he wailed in agony. As he watched, Joe saw Ava being pulled through the blood covered snow and it was spreading all over her and she too screamed at what she now knew was happening.

As she did, new tendrils separated from the ones pulling her husband and latched onto her and instantly pulled and tore fissures in her skin. Joe ran and grabbed at her and did his best to pull the limbs from her but for every one he broke away, another one came to take its place at once and then he felt the grasping of one of the spindly finger of death reaching for his own flesh and he backed away in fright.

The couple was pulled farther away, both of them screaming and oozing blood and Joe couldn't tell what else from their wounds. With tears in his own eyes now, he cocked his revolver and fired two shots. Both Jarrod and Ava died at once as the bullets entered their heads and all of a sudden the whole forest went silent.

The bodies of the couple stopped moving along the ground and nothing moved. Joe stared at what he had done and felt his knees buckle as nausea overcame him. None of the others said anything and after a few moments of silence, the tendrils slipped away along the ground like serpents, almost as soundlessly as they had come.

For a whole minute after they were gone everyone just stood where they were. It had been a much harder shock this time than last and Joe wished at that moment he had been the one to have a bullet through his head. He heard light footsteps come behind him and turned to see Sally. Her face was tear-streaked, but she managed to hold her voice.

"You did the right thing, Joe," she said, putting a hand on his shoulder. He looked in her eyes and nodded and then turned to see what kind of reaction Susan and Sam were having. Susan was weeping but still she nodded in agreement with what Sally had said.

"You saved them from a much worse end," Sam said, "but it can't have been easy for you." Joe nodded at this; it had been the hardest thing he'd ever done in his life. He stood and looked once more at the couple. They were so unrecognisable to the two people he'd first met only a matter of hours before, really. How unlucky they had been to get stuck in Mercy on their way to California. How unlucky all of them had been to be stuck in Mercy for whatever reason had brought them all here.

"We need to try to hole up in the tavern," he said, walking over to Sam and Susan and taking her weight on one side. "I don't ever want to have to do anything like that again." No one made any reply to this, and they set off towards Mercy, leaving the two bodies as they were. Now was not the time for ceremony or tradition.

"What part does Maul have to play in this?" Joe asked Sally when finally they were all ensconced in the tavern.

Himself and Sam had spent the last ten minutes hauling a heavy bed into the main room so Susan could lie down and Sally could tend to her better. Sally looked at Joe oddly at the question.

"Why do you think I might know?" she answered.

"You're as good a bet as anyone I guess," Joe said and then hesitating a moment added, "He did save you after all." Sally's face flushed at this possible inference and her ire rose.

"Probably because I'm the only person in this town who ever showed him the smallest bit of human decency!"

"Take it easy, Sal," Joe said raising his hands. "I'm not accusing you of anything, but if you know anything at all about Maul that might help us here we need to know."

"He doesn't control it," Susan's weak voice rose from the bed. Everyone looked at her.

"What's that Susan?" Sam asked, taking up her hand.

"Whatever it is that's happened to the trees has also happened to Maul. He doesn't control what it does but he can't stop it either."

"How do you know this?" Sam asked.

"I don't, but that's how it looks to me. Maul saved Sally because he feels maybe he owes her that, but he didn't try to save anyone else but that's probably because he knows he can't."

"You could be right, Susan," Joe said looking to Sally to see if she had anything to add to this.

"So he's as much a victim in all this as any of us," she said flatly.

"I guess so," Joe nodded but then thinking more asked of the room, "But why didn't it kill him like it's been trying to with the rest of us?" They were silent at this.

Sally went to the window behind the counter and looked up at the mine entrance where they had been and where the bodies of the two young people still lay out of sight.

"Those poor kids," she said and Joe saw tears drip down her cheeks, a sight he never thought he'd have to see with her. Joe walked over and put a hand on her back and she turned and buried her head into his chest as he wrapped his arms around her. He looked out through the window himself as he comforted her and then he recalled what Sally had said about Maul being up there one day, and his own recollection of seeing the thin white trail from the mine entrance. Was that where this disease or white death had come from? Somewhere deep and forgotten in the earth.

Sally must have felt a change in him for she leaned back and looked at his face and then followed his gaze outside.

"What is it?" she asked.

"I just remembered when I was up there a few days ago looking for Maul, I saw some of this white stuff on the rotten wood that covered the entrance to the mine," he answered. "I'm wondering now if maybe that's where this all started."

"Anything is possible," Sally replied.

"Maybe I should go back up there and take a closer look into the shaft. It can't make things any worse and I might find out something useful?"

Chapter 27

Jeff moved through the deep snowdrifts, his thighs aching with the effort and his body hot beneath the clothes he wore against the cold. All the time since he'd left the group he had been scrutinizing the forest before him and moving away from anything he saw that made it seem like the hue of the trees was lighter than he wanted it to be. He had been looking through squinted eyes for so long that his cheeks were hurting. His ears were alive to every sound outside his own traveling and he constantly stopped to listen for any signs of danger.

After what felt like an hour but was probably in reality only twenty minutes, Jeff had to stop to rest. The uneven terrain and the weight of the wet boots on his feet, coupled with his general lack of shape, conspired to make him feel like a ninety-year-old man who'd smoked a hundred a day for most of his life. He sat on a wide stump and looked around. It was disheartening to think, as Joe had said, that it would be morning before he could even some close to thinking he was safe.

He wished Mouse was with him now. It wouldn't make it any safer — the fact that Mouse was already dead was testament to that, but Jeff felt like he could do with a friend right now. Someone who he didn't even need to talk to but just someone to be here with him, going through the same thing he was. It was hard to believe that such a man like Mouse could be dead and to be killed by, of all things, the forest where he'd spent his whole life. It beggared belief.

"If only you'd finished Maul off like you always wanted to, Mouse, we probably wouldn't be in this mess now," he said with a smile on his face. He'd known all along how scared Mouse had been of the wild Thorndean. Jeff was sure Mouse had always believed Jeff saw him as fearless of the man but it was clear in the changed voice of the huge man anytime he met Maul that he was terrified of him.

"Was it you who killed him, Maul?" he also asked aloud. Was it possible that Maul was somehow part of this forest now, each tree his eyes and his ears for miles all around? The idea that this was even remotely possible set him to walking again. Sleep is what he wanted to do but walk was what he needed to do. It was hard to imagine he would ever feel the comfort of a bed again. He moved off again.

The searing pain of a stitch shocked Jeff's ribs as he walked farther on and he altered his body as he walked to lessen the hurt. This new walking position put strain on new muscles however and soon not only was his back hurting but his lungs stung as he breathed in, a pain that was equal to if not worse than the stitch itself.

Stopping and leaning against a large boulder that cropped out of the ground—and was taller than he was—Jeff breathed shallowly to try to ease his lungs. He gripped a handful of flesh at his side where the stitch was, almost feeling like he held the pain itself within his palm — an old remedy he'd used since he was a child and always found effective. He leaned back on the flat face of the stone and turned his cheek to it to feel the cool surface. It was a moment of bliss compared to anything the last few hours had presented him but it was to be very short-lived.

"Shopkeeper," a growling deep voice said from the depths of the woods. Jeff shot up straight and looked all around, unsure which direction the sound had come from. He cocked his gun and aimed at nothing spinning the barrel from one part of the forest to another.

"Who's there?" Jeff called out. "Where are you?" No answer came and for a few moments the only sound was the rattling of Jeff's gun in his cold shaking hands.

"Shopkeeper," the voice came again. "Run." Jeff turned to where he thought the voice was coming from and aimed his rifle into the darkness. Planting his feet more firmly into the ground, he said,

"I'm through running," the breath falling in thick fast mists from his mouth as his heart raced harder than ever before in his life. "Come on out Maul," he said. "Let's finish this now."

What greeted this response was a low growling noise, deep and gravely and then slowly rising in volume. That horrible noise of the twiggy snaking tendrils came on slowly too but seemed to gather pace as the growling noise turned into a roar of what Jeff could only think of as abject and utter fury. It was a sound so terrifying that his knees rattled and tears fell from his eyes, blurring them badly.

"Show yourself you fucking coward!" he shouted at the top of his voice. The tendril noises grew closer and closer but seemed still to be a distance away and not yet in sight.

Jeff wiped at his eyes in an effort to see better and as he did he was sure something moved, something like he'd seen when they were attacked earlier. He fired off two quick shots and heard the bullets hit home and the roar of furious pain that went with them. As he'd been concentrating on the shape moving, Jeff hasn't noticed the tendrils rush across the ground out of the trees and his legs were suddenly swiped from under him and he fell heavily on his back, the gun clattering off the rock and falling to the ground a couple of feet from him.

Faster than he would have thought possible, he found his body almost completely covered in those awful tightening tendrils and he pressed back as hard as he could against them, hearing some snapping and cracking as he did so. It was all in vain however and he was soon cocooned and could barely move at all.

Then he noticed something he found odd. The tightening had stopped and no part of the tendril seemed to be trying to do him any harm. He only had a moment to wonder why before he heard the heavy footstep of what was once Maul Thorndean coming from within the trees.

"I suppose this is what you've always wanted," Jeff spat at the shape as it loomed over him. "Killing everyone in town?"

As he looked on the creature whose face was so little like that it once wore but enough to know that it was indeed Maul in there, it spoke those same words again, though his time in a lower tone,

"Shopkeeper, run." Jeff didn't know what he meant by this but he knew there was no way he was going to be even walking, let alone running away from this situation. He was about to attempt to spit in Maul's leaning over wooden scaled face when a new thought scampered into his mind — two shots! He'd fired two shots that hit Maul and that was the signal he'd told the others he would raise when he was safely off the mountain.

'They would know you didn't have the time yet to get off the mountain,' he second-guessed himself. But it was also possible that he had found some faster way down wasn't it, a random driver that had somehow gotten through on the road or something similar. He looked to the gun and knew he had to fire once more if only to stop giving the false hope to those back up in Mercy.

The gun was close but his arms were pinned to the ground and time wasn't on his side. Knowing this, he closed his eyes and put all his effort into one huge surge of strength in his right hand — the one closest to the rifle — and pulled free with timbers breaking and snapping as he did. He got hold of the gun just as another tendril shot over and held him down once more, he felt through the hoop and pulled the trigger. The noise was deafening and a clod of earth burst up into the air a few feet away where the bullet made contact. Maul didn't move a muscle, and the tendril crushed in once more.

Jeff looked up at the night sky and held off screaming for as long as he could. It wasn't all that long in the end and no doubt his agonised wails as he was crushed to death would have made up for any misconception the three shots would have fostered in those remaining up the mountain.

Chapter 28

Joe stood at the front door of the Lone Wolf Tavern and looked out at the little town he'd known as home these last years. Never in his life had he felt so hopeless and bereft of ideas. The white death was spreading all around and getting closer to town all the time. It wouldn't be long before the buildings here would be surrounded with bent over vines and trees like the Thorndean place. He wondered how long it would be before that happened. It would not be a pretty end for any of them that was for sure.

The idea of shooting the others now before the horror arrived crossed his mind, but he pushed it away. In the moment like with Ava and Jarrod, he might be able to do it again but not in cold blood; that wasn't in him. He looked down towards his office and thought of trying the radio again. Just as he took the first step, the noise of the door opening behind him halted his progress.

"Where do you think you're going?" Sally said with as close an imitation of her usual smirk as she was able to pull off just then.

"I was going to go over and try the radio one last time."

"Worth a try I suppose," she said, "You want some company walking over."

"Sure."

They walked in silence down the short distance to the sheriff's office and Joe held the door for Sally to go inside.

"Finger crossed," he said leading her to the radio room. Sally showed him her own crossed fingers and looked about the room. She had never been in here before.

Joe fiddled to no avail with the radio for a couple of minutes before giving up. Sally saw his disappointment and didn't bother making any remarks on the radio not working. After a moment he looked at her and said,

"You should get out of here."

"The station?" she asked not sure what else he could be talking about but also not understanding why he would put her out of this building.

"No, Mercy. It looks as though you might be the only one safe to get out. Maul will protect you."

"I can't go and leave the rest of you here," she answered.

"You have to; it's the only way anyone is going to survive." Sally was shaking her head before he even finished talking,

"No, I can't do it," she said. "I can't leave you all like that, especially Susan."

"If you don't get out here, we won't be able to warn anyone about what's happening here."

"Jeff might still get out," she said.

"He might, but wouldn't it be better if two got out rather than none?"

"If you're so sure Maul will protect me, I can leave at any time," she retorted, and it sounded like a child arguing.

At that moment three shots rang out from the forest. Joe and Sally looked at one another.

"Jeff?" Sally said hopefully.

"He can't have gotten down the mountain that quickly," Joe said. They went to the door and listened to the night. There was no more noise.

"He did say he would fire three shots once he was safe," Sally whispered. Joe wanted to think this was what had happened, but he didn't feel it. Then the third shot came and confirmed it. Out of the corner of his eye, he saw Sally's head drop and then heard her weeping. To make things worse, Jeff's tortured screams filled the mountainside air as he died what must have been a gruesome death. Sally gasped at this noise and buried her head in Joe's chest.

"Oh my God!" she sobbed. Joe held her close again and felt the hot sting in his own eyes.

"We better go back to Susan and Sam," he said and ushered her onto the road. Sally moved with him but it was like she suddenly had the frailty of a ninety-year-old woman. He guessed Jeff's death had been the one to send her over the edge and into despair.

There was no doubt by the glum faces and wet eyes on the couple in the tavern that they too had heard Jeff's grisly demise. It was probably all the worse that they had only heard it; their imaginations would conjure up much worse horrors than whatever it was that had actually happened.

The fire was blazing in the hearth now, having been started by Sam since Joe had left the room, and the flames licked high into the chimney. Looking at the room — save the bed that clearly didn't belong — it looked so warm and inviting. You would never guess the pandemonium that was going on outside the cosy tavern. An image of Centrepoint on fire came to mind; the view he'd seen from the top of the mountain and suddenly it made sense to him.

"What are you thinking?" Sam asked him suddenly. "Your face changed just now." The others looked at Joe.

"Earlier, when I went looking for Mouse, I saw from the peak that there was a big fire in Centrepoint," Joe started.

"Centrepoint?" Sam interrupted.

"It's a town about twenty miles away on the other side of the mountain," Susan told him.

"What about it?" Sally asked Joe impatient for him to get on with it.

"I didn't think too much of it at the time, but just now I had the idea that perhaps they are having the same trouble we are."

"The trees?" Susan asked.

"Yes," Joe nodded.

"You think it could have spread that far from either here to there or the other way round?" Sally asked.

"I do," Joe said. "But that's not the point. I think they found a way to fight it, a very obvious way as it turns out."

"Fire!" Sam said.

"They set their town on fire?" Susan seemed doubtful.

"I doubt they saw they had a choice," Joe said, "If the same thing is happening there as here can you blame them for getting extreme."

"So you want to set the forest on fire?" Sally asked making sure she had a handle on what they were talking about.

"Fire kills wood," Sam said shrugging his shoulders.

"I think it's our only choice," Joe said.

"And what if that doesn't work?" Susan asked.

"Well, in that case, we will be no worse off than we are now."

"So how do we do this?" Sam said with an eagerness that had been lacking in everyone for some hours now.

"Gasoline," Joe said. "We've got some in Jeff's garage and then whatever we can syphon from the cars that are still around."

"Let's get to it then!" Sam said and then looking at Susan said, "We'll get out of this yet!"

"Susan," Sally said, "You'll have to stay here on your own a while; it will take as many hands as we can get to spread the gas all around town and start the fires." Susan nodded.

"I only wish I could help," she said casting her eyes to the bedsheets.

"We're going to need to split up for this," Sally said then to Joe. "No arguments this time." Joe nodded; she was right. They would have to cover as much ground as they could as fast as they could and get a circle of fire around the town.

Sam leaned in and kissed Susan.

"We'll be back soon," he said. "Don't worry."

"I'll be fine," she said and then added, "Good luck to you all."

"Let's go," Joe said. "We don't have much time."

Chapter 29

There were ten five-gallon drums of gasoline in Jeff Sorkin's garage.

"Plenty to get a fire going," Sam said looking at them.

"Let's hope it lights well in all this snow," Joe said trying to calculate how much of a fire this haul might fuel.

"I say we head uphill first as it seems to be coming down the mountain faster than coming up it," Sally said.

"I think we should have two up and one down," Sam said. "Best to head off what's coming up too, I say."

"I agree with that," Joe said, "Sally can you start downhill?" Sally nodded.

"Probably best we start at the points we need to get to farthest from here first so the journeys for more gas are getting shorter rather than longer," Sam said. Joe nodded at this too and wondered briefly if there was any merit to starting some fires along the way with small Molotov cocktails? He concluded that it would take too long to make even a few of these up and dismissed the idea.

"What happens if it doesn't light up, or if the wind changes and blows the flames back at us in town?" Sally asked. Joe thought about this a moment and then answered sombrely,

"It will either kill it, or kill us, but either way it will be over for us."

There was a moment of silence as they each pondered this before Sam, getting more buoyant by the minute it seemed smiled and said,

"Well let's hope it doesn't turn back on us," and he picked up one of the drums. He immediately put it back down. "That's too heavy to carry any real distance!"

"We'll have to pour it into something else," Sally said looking around.

"I've got a couple of half-filled containers in the jeep, we can use that to get you started Sally," Joe said. "And we'll figure out what to do here." Sally nodded and set off.

"I'll get it myself," she said. "I assumed the jeep in unlocked?"

"It is," Joe answered. "Take care and call if you need us."

"I'll be fine," she said stopping at the door. "I have my guardian angel, remember?" She winked and then disappeared out into the night. Joe smiled and then saw Sam was looking at him perplexed,

"What was that about?" he asked.

"I'll tell you when this is all over," Joe said and he set about looking for something to pour some of the gasoline into. Sam stood there a moment longer at this answer before shrugging and getting on with the task in hand himself.

All they could find were three small jerry-cans. They filled them from one drum and they poured some more from a second drum into the first one so both drums were a little lighter than when they started.

"I'm going to get the jeep," Joe said, "We can put these in the back and drive up the road a little to get started."

While Joe was gone, Sam moved as much as he could closer to the door. All the time he was thinking 'if this works, Susan and I can finally make a go of things.' It was something worth risking his life for to his mind and not just a last gasp effort to survive. He'd wanted nothing more in his life than he wanted to be with Susan and all today had done despite the horrors he'd both seen and endured was to solidify that opinion.

"We'll do this Susan," he said, and he felt right and good was on his side. This was a plan that was going to work.

Both men watched the trees like hawks as they slowly moved down the road in Joe's jeep.

"A couple hundred yards will do it?" Joe said.

"Best not to go too far," Sam answered. They had decided on getting into the jeep, as the road was a separation in the fire line they were hoping to create it would probably be best to start two fires on either side of the road to get things started. Joe pulled up in the middle of the road a hundred yards past Susan's house.

"I'll start on this side," Joe said. "Keep your eyes open." Sam nodded, and they both got out and took a half-filled drum each from the back of the jeep. They looked at one another once more and then set about their work.

"Try to get the fire going with as little gas as you can," Sam said, "We can make it go a lot farther then."

"Good point," Joe said nodding before they went to opposite sides of the road to begin their work.

Joe stood by the tree closest to the road and listened carefully and looked around for any sign of attack. Hefting the gas can up he undid the lid and splashed some on the bark of the tree. Then, taking a step back he sheltered himself from the wind and struck a match and pressed it to the tree, ready to pull his hand away instantly if it took flame faster than he thought it would. To his great dismay, the first match was snuffed out on contact with the wet of the gas. He had another idea at once however and pulling his handkerchief from his pocket put a little of the gas on it and then held a new flame beneath it. It took longer than he would have thought but soon the cloth was alight. He held it away from his body and let the flames press against the tree. This time the tree did go on fire but it was small and didn't look like it had much life in it. He felt that it would simply burn the gasoline of the bark and then die out.

"It's too wet!" he called out to Sam, and he felt stupid at having the idea in the first place. It had been snowing for days; how could he have possibly expected the wet trees to go up in a huge inferno?

"Shit! Shit! Shit!" he heard Sam reaching the same conclusion.

It was gutting for Joe but he could hear in Sam that it was even worse for him and he knew why. It had been a long time since he had been romantically involved with anyone but he could still recall that feeling at the start of love. It must be a terrible thing to have it snatched away from you just when you thought you might be able to hang on to it.

Joe looked at the tree before him thinking of a way to make this endeavour work. He looked up at the branches and thought about setting those alight but they were snow covered and would be even wetter through than the trunks. The ray of hope that this fire had sparked was diminishing quickly and it was hard not to let it defeat him there and then.

"There must be something we can do!" he called out to Sam.

After a moment's more silence, Sam walked across the road. On seeing this, Joe moved too and met his near the jeep.

"There is something we can do with fire," Sam said but his face wasn't showing any great confidence in whatever it was he was thinking.

"What?"

"Those vines, or branches or whatever it is that it uses to attack us," Sam said. "They are dry and brittle."

"Those would burn with the gas," Joe said following his idea.

"Except, the only time we see those is when they are trying to kill us." Joe thought about this and it was true that they had not seen these tendrils in a relaxed state anywhere. It seemed like they could come from any tree at any time.

"We need to go to where the white starts and burn from there," he said, already knowing the difficulty this would present. Sam nodded.

"And at that point, we would be opening ourselves up for a very bad end if we couldn't get the fire started quick enough."

"Even if we did get it started, it might be too late to get away," Joe said.

"We need to think of a way of spreading the gas fast once the first ignition takes place."

They stood in silence thinking on this. Joe was hoping Sam would come up with an idea as he was finding it hard to think clearly himself and nothing practical was coming to mind. He tried to tell himself that this was just his inner critic coming to the fore, not letting him come up with ideas as his last to burn wet trees had been so idiotic. Still no idea came.

"We better go down to Sally," he said. "She's probably found out this idea isn't going to work by now."

Neither man said anything on the way back through Mercy to find Sally. Both thought hard on finding a solution to their problem of spreading the fire quickly. Joe's thoughts went to wishing, and he imagined one of those fire planes for putting out fires dropping gallons of water only this time they would be dropping gasoline on the trees to fuel the fires on the ground.

"There she is," Sam said pointing and Joe looked at saw first some smoke and then a smouldering heap in the low branches of a tree. Sally had turned to face them at the sound of the jeep approaching. Vexation was plain to see on her face and it was a light moment for the two men as they smiled in her shared annoyance.

"It's not taking; there's been too much snow!" she said as they got out of the jeep.

"We know, we had the same trouble," Joe said.

"So what in hell are we supposed to do now?" Sally said looking from one to the other.

"We're working on a new plan," Joe said.

"Which is?" Sally pressed him.

"The white trees and the limbs that have attacked us seem to be dry and brittle so we are trying to come up with a way to set those alight without getting killed in the process," Sam answered. She looked to Joe then as if to see if this was really the case and said,

"That doesn't sound all that doable to me."

"We'll think of something," Joe said. "We have to."

Chapter 30

"**B**randy is what we need after that!" Sally declared as they came back into the tavern's main room once more. They'd decided they might think better indoors than standing out in the cold and they would also have the benefit of Susan's brain too if she hadn't slipped into a fever while they'd been gone.

"I wasn't expecting you all back so soon," Susan said with clear alarm in her voice as she scanned to see they had all come back. "What happened?"

"We didn't think it through," Joe said. "It's much too wet out there to start any kind of fire that would do real damage."

"Oh," Susan said as Sam got to her bedside and took her hand.

"We're coming up with a new plan, though," he said to her. "We can probably still burn it but we have to get to the diseased white trees to do it."

"How?" she asked in alarm.

"That's what we're back in here to figure out," Sally said, banging four glasses down on the counter and unscrewing the top of the brandy bottle. She poured four large measures as the others watched her; the glow of the fire in the liquid through the glass causing it to look like the most homely and inviting thing in the world right then.

Coming from behind the bar, Sally handed a glass to each of them and raised her glass.

"To good ideas," she said. The others raised their own glasses in reply.

"No idea is too stupid to mention," Joe said after they had all downed a swallow of the warm brandy. "You never know what will spark the right idea in someone else."

No one said anything for a while as they searched silently for a solution.

"Is there anything we could use like a sling shot to fire something towards it?" Susan asked sheepishly. "I know it sounds silly but maybe there is."

"It would be ideal if there was," Joe said. "but I can't think of anything that would do the trick."

"I was thinking the same thing, like using the timing belt from one of the cars but I can't think of a way to make it work."

"What about something else we could use to spray it somehow, from the bed of a truck or something?" Susan said, and this was when Joe's mind lit up with an idea. The others all talked at once fobbing this idea off as fancy but wishing there was a way to use it. Joe said nothing at first but tried to follow the thread of his thought to its natural conclusion. When it got there, it would have been much easier for him to forget about than to resign himself to it and tell the others.

"There is something we can use to spray the gas," he said and everyone fell silent and looked at him. He looked back at them with the fondness of a father and tried to think of one final twist that would mean he could carry his plan out alone but it didn't come to him. "I think," he said. "That Sally and Susan should take one of the vehicles and use the road as far down to Emerson as they can get."

"What about you two?" Sally asked before he could go on.

"I'll get to that," Joe said holding out a placating hand. "You should get out then and..." then the idea he'd been looking for came to him. There was a way he could do this alone after all. "Scrap that, Sam will be going with you too."

"What are you talking about?" Sam asked.

"I think Maul will protect Sally as much as he can," Joe said, "and if you are all in the same car as she is then he will have to protect you by default." Joe then turned to Sally almost excited with his new idea.

"We're going to need all of your bottles, Sally, both the full and the empty, and every other glass container we can get our hands on in the next ten minutes," Joe said, an excited edge to his voice.

"What have you got in mind?" Sally asked.

"Just like we already planned," Joe said winking, "Fire."

"What do you need all the bottles for?" Sam asked.

"He wants to get close enough to throw them at the white trees and start a fire that way," Susan said. "That's it isn't it?" she asked looking at Joe.

"In a nutshell," he answered.

"How were you planning on getting all these bottles up to the white tree line on your own?" Sam asked.

"I don't," Joe said. "But I will need some help before you all leave."

"What makes you think we're just going to leave you here alone?" Sam asked.

"My duty is to you people," Joe said. "Your duty Sam, is to get Susan out of here safely, and your duty Sally is to go with them and hopefully be able to use whatever influence you have on Maul to keep you all safe."

"Why can't you come with us then?" Sally asked, not bothering to assert the lack of influence she felt she had over Maul.

"We need as many fires as we can get going at once for this to spread the way we need it to. That means you will be tossing flaming bottles into the white trees as you go and I will be getting as large a fire as I can going at this side of things."

Joe looked about the room and though he could see it wasn't sitting well with any of the others; they could at least see where he was coming from. Susan began to cry again and this time Sam only stood motionless, his face blank as he silently accepted Joe was right.

"You still haven't explained how you plan to get the bottles to the trees on your own," Sam said.

"I don't intend getting too much up there," Joe said as his plan solidified in his mind. "I'm only going to bring a few bottles up and toss them around, unlit."

"What good will that do?" Sally asked.

"They will go up when the fire reaches them and give it a little boost in the process," Joe answered.

"I still don't understand what you're planning to do," Sam said. Joe looked around at their expectant faces and for a moment he felt like he would not be able to talk such was the lump in his throat.

"This is the plan," he began. "We get all the bottles filled with gas and stuff, some with torn up sheets for firebombs. I'll get as many as I can up on to the roof of the tavern — I'll explain that bit in a minute. As you drive down the mountain I need you, Sam, to light the ones you bring with you and throw them all around in the white trees on either side of the road to get the flames going." They all nodded along that they understood so far and Joe went on. "While you're doing that I will spread some of the bottles and gas cans around the outskirts of the town and then come back here to the tavern."

"Those vines will just crush the car like they did mine," Sam said.

"Maybe," Joe admitted. "But perhaps the fire will cause them to either flee or else confuse it somehow. And then there's Maul."

"I don't put too much stock in Maul Thorndean helping anyone," Susan said bitterly.

"I've seen him save Sally already," Joe said. "I think we all have. We just have to hope he's able and willing to do it again."

"And if we can't get through?" Susan asked her eyes hot with an anger Joe knew was borne of fear.

"Then you'll be no worse off than you are here, but at least you will have tried to survive." Susan didn't say anything back to this.

"Why do you need to get things up on the roof?" Sally asked to bring the talk back to Joe's plan.

"That's where I'm going to start the fire from," he answered.

"You mean you're going to let the white come all the way to the tavern first?" Sam asked.

"That's right. There are some spray cans around and I'm going to use those to spray the trees from the roof once they are white and then set them alight. Once that's started I'm going to throw out those firebomb bottles in every direction as far as I can. My hope is that all of these fires will begin to join up and then when they reach the bottles and cans I leave around the place they should explode and send fire in all directions, spreading it even farther and faster."

"You think you can kill it like that?" Sally asked.

"It's the only way I can imagine it can be done, but there are no guarantees," Joe answered.

"You think there's any way you can survive being in the middle of all that?" Sally asked now and her face too flashed with anger.

"I don't intend surviving," he answered tapping his gun. "But I hope to take this evil with me. Like I said, this is my duty, it comes with being a police officer."

"We won't let you do it," Sally said. "Will we?" She looked to Susan and Sam.

"Sally," Joe said before either could answer. "I know this is very hard, but this is how it has to be. If I go with you three and we don't make it, this thing could live on to kill who knows how many more people. This way, we have a slight chance of you getting out to warn Emerson about this thing, and also a real chance to stop it in its tracks."

"A slight chance," Sally said sullenly.

"Our only chance," Joe corrected her.

The wind sounded through the door and the fire crackled in the grate as they all looked around the room for what would be one of the last times. It was hard to think of Mercy gone but that was the most likely outcome this night.

"If we're going through with this, we better get started now," Sally said shedding one bulbous tear and wiping it away with her sleeve.

"Let's light up the night," Sam said defiantly.

Chapter 31

Sam and Joe moved all the gas to the tavern as the two women filled the bottles and cut up the sheets and soaked them. It was grim work, and the smell was powerful enough they had to open the window to let some cool clean air in.

"Don't be too careful with that," Sally said to Susan. "This building will go up in flames too so we can afford to have some on the floor."

"I'm sorry you're losing your business," Susan said looking sadly at her.

"I'm sorry we're all losing our homes," Sally replied, "but that's a small price to pay if we get out of this alive." The last was said in the most upbeat tone Sally had been able to muster for what felt like a lifetime but in reality was only a few hours, a day at most. She could see Susan's eyes on her and she knew there was a question behind them. "What is it?" Sally asked.

"Do you think Maul did save you specifically?" Sally thought for a moment before answering,

"It certainly looked that way," she said.

"I suppose you were the only one who ever was kind to him."

"I suppose," Sally said dipping another rag in gasoline and planting it in the neck of a bottle. "But then, I'm the only one around here who he never gave cause to treat him any different." Susan nodded slightly at this answer but said nothing more on the subject.

Sam came in again and puffed out air in exhaustion.

"Joe's gone off planting some of his bombs and he wants me to start putting some of these bottles in the car," he said.

"Which car are we taking?" Susan asked.

"I suppose Jeff's truck is the most rugged of what's left," Sam shrugged. The two women nodded in agreement and Sam took up a box of bottles and went outside.

"Have you noticed how much, I don't know — happier doesn't seem like the right word, but..."

"How changed Joe is since he came up with this plan?" Sally finished for Susan who nodded that this was indeed what she had been trying to say. "I have. I think his plan has given him a sense of purpose he's probably never had before — and a determination to see it through to boot."

"You can see in his eyes that his mind won't be changed," Susan said.

"He's a brave man," Sally said. "Foolish," she added, "but brave." They both smiled.

"Brave? Someone talking about me again?" Sam said joking as he re-entered. The two women extended their smiles to him.

"How many of these are we going to take with us?" Sally asked, referring to the bottles.

"I suppose two boxes will do it if we're going to leave enough for Joe."

"Right; you carry this second box out and I'll get up and sweep some of the snow off the roof," Sally said getting up.

"How are you going to get up there?" Sam asked in surprise.

"There's stairs down the hall with a door than opens out. The roof is mainly flat up there and slopes around the edges. I don't know who designed the place or why but I've always kept a yard brush up there for heavy snow in case the roof might cave in one day. I go up every couple of days when it's like this; I was only up there day before last." Susan and Sam looked at one another with amusement; neither of them had known any of this before.

"I guess you never really know what's going in other people's lives, even in a town as small as Mercy," Susan smiled.

Sally pulled her coat on and took a swig from a brandy bottle for warmth and then headed down the corridor to the narrow steep stairs that lay behind one door at the end. To look from either end of this corridor, you would never know this door was any different to the others that led into either bedrooms or a bathroom.

A draft rushed out at her as she opened the door and she saw snow fall in through the cracks in the boards of the trapdoor at the top of the stars. The brush was on the first step and she grabbed hold of it as she passed on the way up. It clattered noisily on the hollow steps as Sally dragged it behind her.

At the top, the door was at a forty-five degree angle and she stopped a few steps before it. Bringing the brush past her body she held it by the head and banged four heavy blows on the door from the inside to loosen the snow that would be sitting on it by now. She heard the fall of some snow and then the sliding noise as more fell away moments later. She unhitched the bolt and leaned her shoulder against the cold wood and pushed using the brush against the steps now for extra support.

The door opened up to a black night sky and her misty breath filled her view for a moment as she stepped through the doorway. She saw at once that the white tree line had come down the mountain by a significant distance and it wouldn't be long before it was reaching the outskirts of town.

Just as she was about to start sweeping to clear a space for Joe up here, she heard something in the trees about fifty yards from her. She looked for the source of the sound but couldn't see anything. The noise kept on and she wished now she'd brought her gun up here. Stepping closer to the edge of the roof, she peered into the darkness and listened more carefully.

"Who's there?" she called out. "That you, Maul?" The noise stopped, and then she saw something moving in the trees.

"It's only me!" Joe called back stepping into a small clearing and waving. "I'll be back inside in another ten minutes!"

"Alright," Sally waved back. "You just be careful."

"Don't worry about me. You just be sure you three are ready to leave when I get back. This thing is getting closer to town by the minute."

"I see, that," Sally said and then realizing she was distracting him said, "Go on, get your job done and get back here to us." She waved him away as she said this and he made a gesture that he understood and he disappeared once more.

Sally returned to her own task and swept a mound of snow near the edge and watched with childish delight as it fell and pounded ten feet below. She turned to do more and glanced once again to where Joe had just been and froze in horror. There standing the same clearing as before was that wooden deformed creature that had once been Maul Thorndean!

Chapter 32

Joe walked back past the gas can he'd placed against a tree glancing at it and imagining the explosion it would make and trying to estimate how many trees would be in its radius. Along with those he had already placed and what he was planning to throw and spray from the roof of the tavern, he was thinking it was going to be a sizable blaze and one that was very likely to spread quickly through the rest of the dry wood. He smiled at the thought of it; this could work.

"Joe!" a shrill scream shattered his thoughts, and he stopped cold and looked back, though he couldn't see it anymore, to the tavern. It had been Sally's voice, not as he'd ever heard it, but he knew it was her. "Maul is right beside you, run!" came the fearful tear-filled voice. Joe spun to look where he'd come from but saw nothing moving. Then a sound like a huge animal thrashing through the underbrush came from the darkness and Joe didn't wait to see whether or not or not Sally had been right. He fled as fast as he could towards his parked Jeep, a hundred yards away from his starting point.

As he ran, he did his best to unholster his gun, but something that was so simple and second nature to him was now causing him all sorts of trouble as he bounced and tripped and jumped through the hard terrain to escape.

"Run!" a deep growling voice came from behind him and seemed so close that Joe actually jumped in startled fear as he heard it. Fortunately, in this leap of sorts, his holster came undone, and he pulled the gun easily from it. Checking the ground in front him for a split second he then looked back over his shoulder and saw branches and bushes getting pushed and pulled as Maul came through after him. It was too hard in that brief glimpse to see what part of the moving was actually the body of Maul but Joe fired away, three shots in a small arc that he knew at least one of them would land home in the creature.

A roar of angered pain rang out behind him and Joe knew he'd hit it somewhere. The noise from behind didn't seem to be slowing, however, and Joe decided not to waste any more of his precious lead in distance on trying again.

"Run!" the deep growl came again. He couldn't be sure but Joe felt that perhaps the voice sounded farther away now, and this gave him one last surge of hope that pressed down into his legs and he sprinted the last few feet to the jeep. He'd left the key in the ignition and he glad of it as he set the car in motion and sped down the hill to Mercy.

Pulling up outside the tavern, he jumped out and looked up the road behind him. There was no sign of either Maul or those fearsome tendrils anywhere.

"Are you alright?" Sally's concerned voice came from above him. Joe looked up and smiled with relief.

"I'm fine, thanks for the warning, though."

"Did you get what you needed to do done?" she asked.

"Not all of it, but I think there's enough to do what I need. I'll be able to throw the bottles farther down the hill than up it too, so that's a plus."

"About the only plus in all of this," Sally smiled.

"What are you doing on the roof, anyway?" Joe asked.

"Cleaning it up a little so you won't be slipping all over the place when you come up here."

"Well, thanks for that, but I think it's time you lot got going."

Sally's face broke at this and she couldn't meet his eye any more. She nodded and said,

"I'll come down now." Her voice monotone with sadness.

Joe took a deep breath, gathered more of the gas cans from the jeep and carried them inside. The three of them were in the main room of the tavern all looking at him when he came in. It was a moment that once more very seriously tested the resolve of Joe Moorefield and he knew he had to get them out of here as quickly as possible — while also keeping himself busy until they were gone — if he was going to get through this without crying.

"Sam, I need you to help me get the rest of the gas on the roof while Sally gets Susan into the car and gathers some blankets and food for your way down," he said and as abruptly as he had started talking he pushed through the door into the corridor that led to the stairs to the roof. He'd just made it into the corridor when a tear escaped and rolled down his cheek. He was glad none of them had seen this and as soon as he was on the roof, he put down the cans and wiped his face to obliterate any trace.

Looking out over the forest, he saw that the white was encroaching on the town from above but below it was still a bit off. It was oddly beautiful and Joe was sure he would have felt it so had he not seen what this white death had been all about. Footsteps on the stairs drew his attention and Sam came out onto the roof with a large heavy box of bottles.

"Where do you want there?" he asked.

"Just here in the middle," Joe said, thinking a little more on the task he would soon carry out. He would use all sides of the building so piling everything in the centre was probably the best idea. Sam put the box down and straightened up.

"You sure you won't come with us?" he said. Joe shook his head slowly.

"I can't explain it, Sam," he said, "but I feel that if I'm not here to do this, things could get a whole hell of a lot worse."

"I don't feel right leaving you here."

"I don't feel right leaving you to try to get those women off this mountain, but this is what we got to do. The alternative is that we all die in this building tonight and this thing, whatever it is, just goes on existing and killing anyone who sets foot on the mountain afterwards."

"Why did you come to Mercy, anyway?" Sam asked after a brief pause.

"I came here to get away from it all," Joe sighed. "I've enjoyed living here; I think the few years I've been in Mercy have been the best few for a long, long time, perhaps my whole life."

"It is a great place," Sam said. "Or was, anyway," he corrected himself. "I had a whole future mapped out here; it sounds silly when I only managed to ask Susan out on a date a few days ago."

"That future can still happen," Joe assured him. "Just not here."

"Maybe."

Joe made for the trap door.

"We better get the rest of the gas up here and the spray cans."

They walked down the narrow stairs in silence each thinking of what might have been had life gone on as it always had — up to now. When they came back into the main room of the tavern Susan and Sally turned to them and Sally, with intent said,

"There has to be some kind of goodbye," she walked to the counter where there sat open a bottle of champagne and four flutes.

"I didn't know you had anything so fancy behind there," Joe said.

"There's never been an event I ever thought worthy of busting it out," Sally smiled thinly. She poured and handed out the glasses and they all stood there holding them.

"Well, I suppose first thing we ought to wish each other is luck in what we are about to try," Joe said holding up his glass.

"Good luck to all of us," Sally said raising her glass.

"Good luck," both Susan and Sam said at the same time and they all chinked glasses and drank.

"I really want to say how much I've appreciated how easy a job you all gave me here," Joe said. "I've barely done a day's work since I got started."

"Well you've more than made up for that in the last couple of days," Sam said and they all smiled and for a moment. It didn't feel like the horror of the night was hanging over them.

"To lazy public servants!" Sally cried, and they all laughed and touched glasses and drank once more.

"Let's leave the goodbyes on laughter," Susan said, and it was an idea they all agreed on wholeheartedly.

Chapter 33

Sally pulled Jeff's truck out of the parking spot slowly and looked at Mercy and her beloved tavern one more time. Tears had been coming and going in her eyes since Joe thought up his plan but fresh ones came now and they felt the worse of all so far. Susan was in the passenger seat and she too was crying as she gazed upon the house she'd called home all of her life. She had the photograph Sam had taken from her bedside clutched against her chest as it heaved with her sobbing.

Sam in the back of the truck had been through enough this evening that he didn't care a damn for the town and he was just looking forward to doing as much damage as he could with the fire bombs he had all around him in the bed. The only thing he was worried about was that some of them might break and a fire could start in the truck. He felt better than he had for hours now that they were finally doing something he considered solid. No matter what happened this nightmare would be over in the next half an hour. He glanced up at the roof of the tavern but he wasn't able to see Joe.

As they drove out of town down the hill towards the back road to Emerson, Sally looked in the rear-view mirror and saw that the white of the trees was now in Mercy. Joe would be dead very soon, there was no escaping that idea, but for now she had the lives of this young couple to take into consideration as her first priority.

"Thank you Joe," she whispered unheard by Susan over the roar of the truck's rattling engine.

She didn't drive with any haste and didn't see any point in doing so. If this was going to work, it was going to work, and getting to the point where they were likely to be attacked — wherever that might be — faster would not have any bearing on the outcome.

Three bangs on the roof of the cabin rang out and startled both Susan and her until Sam's voice came over the noise.

"The trees are all white on both sides of the road just ahead," he shouted. "Take it as steady as you can from there unless something happens."

"Alright," Sally shouted back looking at the road ahead. It was as Sam saw, the white death as Joe had called it spread out on both sides of the road not three hundred yards from Mercy now.

"I didn't think it would be so close yet," Susan said staring out as they passed the first white trees.

"Keep you gun aimed out the window, Susan," Sam shouted. Susan looked to Sally and then to the gun in her own hand.

"Better do it," Sally said. "Maul is the only thing probably worth shooting at and if he doesn't help us like we hope you might have to shoot him." Susan nodded and getting a firm grip on the handle rested the barrel on the open window.

"I'm going to start throwing these bottles in," Sam called out. Sally watched the road closely as she tried to maintain as smooth a pass as possible for Sam to launch from.

Moments later she heard a smash and turning to her right saw the trunk of a tree light up in flames.

"Is it working!" Sally asked turning her attention back to the road. Susan leaned her head out the window and looked back and saw with joy that there was a fire going.

"It looks like it!" she said just as another explosion and a fire started off to their left.

"Woo-hoo; they're burning!" Sam's triumphant voice came from behind them.. Sally smiled and glanced out as fires began on either side of the surrounding road. It looked like Joe's plan was working and that even if none of them were to get off this mountain alive tonight, they might at least be taking this thing along with them.

"Do you think it will spread?" she called out the window to Sam.

"I do," he called back. "The ones that have been hit are burning much better than I would have hoped!"

"I hope the whole forest burns to the ground!" Susan said, getting caught up in their excitement and feeling the sharp pain in her ribs tear through her once more. She cried out in pain and Sally looked at her,

"What is it?" she asked thinking something new had happened that she hadn't seen.

"Nothing," Susan assured her. "Just the pain from earlier. I was just getting used to it and it flared up again there."

They continued on at this pace with Sam tossing out the bottles at intervals he thought would best suit their purpose.

It really was looking good for the forest fire part of the plan at least, but the real danger to them would come very soon.

"We're not far from where my truck was crushed," Sam called down. "I don't know if the trees will still be across the road the way they were earlier."

"That's where we have to hope Maul comes in," Sally said. She was nervous now and very happy that she was the one driving so she had something to occupy both her body and her mind.

"This is where it attacked me," Susan said, looking out the window at the spot where she thought her life had come to an end. It was odd how long ago that seemed when in fact in had been no time at all. Sally reached out and squeezed the younger woman's leg.

"Now it's our turn to attack it back," she said.

"The road's still blocked!" Sam shouted in dismay and Sally looked back to the road and saw the white wall of tendrils and branches that spread from either side of the road and met in intricate tangles in the middle.

"What's that at the side of the road?" Sally said, seeing something large but unidentifiable teetering at the edge of the ditch. Susan squinted and then knew what it was.

"It used to be Sam's truck," she said.

"Holy shit!" Sally said, unable to contain it. Though she'd heard both Sam and Joe tell of the damage these trees had done to the vehicles earlier, it was a whole other thing to see the carnage with your own eyes. How on earth had it been possible that Sam was still alive?

"I know," Susan murmured in awe at the wreckage.

Sally was looking ahead at the blockage and it didn't look like there was any life or movement in it. The idea crossed her mind of trying to simply drive through it but she thought she better ask Sam what he thought first.

"Sam!" she called out the window. "What do you think we should do here?"

"I've been thinking all the way down here that if it was still blocked when we got here the only choice is to get out and start a fire and hope we can push through when it weakens the wall."

"You want me to pull up close to it?" she asked just to clarify.

"I suppose so, just far back enough that you will be able to get a bit of a running start for crashing through when the time comes."

"What if we get attacked while the fire is starting, or while we are waiting?" Susan asked.

"We just have to hope that doesn't happen," Sally said as she eased down the gears and stopped the car. The headlights beamed on the blockage, it looked almost like a giant wicker basket had been placed in their way. The both felt and heard Sam move to the side of the bed and jump down crumping heavily into the snow. He came to Susan's window.

"I'm going to go start a couple of fires," he said. "If anything happens you get out of here without hesitation, don't worry about me, just go."

"Just get going and get back here as fast as you can," Sally said nervously. She had the feeling that something was most probably going to happen while they were here and she felt bad that she half hoped Maul would not come to her aid like everyone else thought he would. She couldn't explain even to herself why she felt this way, but it was there all the same.

"You're right," Sam said, and he leaned in and kissed Susan who grabbed hold of him to her.

Sam waited a moment and then pulled away. He looked at them both and went to the back for more gas and walked towards the trees.

Chapter 34

When Joe heard the engine of the truck start up, it was the hardest thing not to go to the side of the building where he would be able to see them and wave goodbye. He knew the reason, and he wasn't ashamed to admit to himself that it would have quite possibly been too difficult and there was a huge chance he would have chickened out of his plan and ran down to get into the truck with them. He stood listening to the sound of the tires on the snow.

The roof sagged with the weight of the gasoline and spray tanks but Joe was sure it would hold. It would get lighter by the minute after all as he went about his work. Joe would just have to be careful not to slip on the depression or spill any of the gasoline which would make it even more slippery again and could seriously hamper his speed when the time came for action. Which was to be soon judging by how close the whitest trees were now. Glancing over his shoulder, he saw downslope the rear red lights of the truck with the others.

"You better help them Maul," he said bitterly. He knew he'd never know if they made it or not and that was a shame, but on the scale of things tonight, it wasn't the worst one.

He looked down over the tops of the trees and though it was hard to be sure he would bet that the white was getting much closer on that side too. No time to dwell on it, he thought, there's still work to do. He went back and took up the spray cans and filled the gas and carried one to opposite sides of the roof and placed them down. He saw from the upslope side that he could probably start spraying now and most of it would hit an infected tree but he decided to wait for as long as he could. Let the white come and bend to the building like he'd seen up at the Thorndean place and then hit it hard for all he was worth.

The thought of this felt good, but it also spawned a new idea he hadn't thought of up to now. He looked down on to the street and saw his jeep parked outside the tavern beside Sally's old jalopy. Up a little was Susan's recovered car and over at Jeff's old garage was the out of operation car that had belonged to the young couple who had been unfortunate enough to pass through this place.

He rushed down the stairs with one of the spray cans with a fresh idea boiling in the front of his brain. He jumped into his jeep and drove it up the road and parked at an angle on the verge of the road just short of where the ground dipped into the trees. He got out and sprayed the inside of the car with gas and then lit a match and held it to the now wet seat. A small fire started, and he leaned in and blew on it to spread it. When he thought it looked like it was self-sustaining, he took off the handbrake and using the door and the frame of the jeep he used all his strength to push it over the verge and then jumped clear as it rolled a few feet into the trees. Some of the trunks snapped and broke and then as he'd hoped branches and vines reached down and pick up the car to crush it. Joe didn't wait around to see if this new plan would work completely but set off back down the hill and took Sally's car.

He drove back, and this time went over the verge in the car and jumped clear as it tipped over. It didn't roll down the hill but teetered there, but this would be good enough he thought, perhaps even better if he could get the car to explode before the trees crushed it. He sprayed this one too and set it alight and then ran back down to get Susan's car.

All the while he was doing this, the horrible screeching crunching noise rang out as the car was pulverized and cubed. Joe was just about at Susan's car when there was a loud bang and the sound of sparks flying. He turned and saw that the car's gas tank had exploded and that some of the tendrils and branches were on fire but not as bad as he could have hoped. Still, every flame was important, and that wasn't going to stop him. He knew the others might do more damage than this.

"Thank God we live in such an isolated place and everyone leaves their keys in their ignition!" he said, smiling as he got into Susan's car. He let the car roll into the ditch to the side of her house and set it alight there. That would soon set the house burning too, if the larger fire Joe was hoping to spread didn't get there first.

Lastly, he pushed Jarrod's car to the middle of the road, set it alight and let it off down the slope. He didn't really care where it ended up when it went off the road, so long as it was into some trees and it was still on fire. He watched it and saw it was staying on the road a lot longer than he thought it would, but even if it kept in a straight line, the road didn't and it would go off soon enough. He walked back to the tavern and to conserve some of his breath and wondered briefly where Alan Carey's car was.

Joe was back on the roof before he heard Jarrod's car crashing down the hill a ways. He couldn't see it so he didn't know it if was serving its purpose but he knew it was in the trees now and with a full gas tank it was going to blow when the big fire got there. As he looked down the hill, he saw five lines of smoke rising into the night sky, and then more and more. Sam must have gotten flames going. It was looking good from where Joe stood and he only wished he could see flames already. The white death was in Mercy now from all sides.

Rushing to the centre of the roof Joe filled the spray tank once more and went to the uphill side of the building. The trees and stretching limbs — slow now, not like the vicious tendrils — reached out for the building walls. Joe sprayed furiously, moving up and down the length of the ledge and getting as good a soaking of the dry white wood as he could. He did this until the can was empty and then got one of the unused sections of ripped sheets and dabbed it some and set it alight.

When it flamed he went to the edge and leaned over and placed it gently onto one of the limbs hoping it would catch fire to the gas he'd sprayed about.

WHOOSH! Flames ripped up at his face and Joe had to fall away back onto the ceiling, his eyes burning from the heat and the smell of his singed eyebrows and even nose hairs filling his head.

"Fuck!" he said pressing his hands into his eyes to lessen the pain. It had gone up way faster than he thought it would.

It was like how people always warn that it can happen but it never does. He sat up and looked, and through blurry eyes could see that flames were licking up over the height of the building and it had already spread some. It was a great start!

Joe jumped up but as he did he felt a terrific pain in his left arm as he used it to get up. He fell back down on his side and held the arm out. What he saw was horrible. His sleeve was torn and ragged but burned and looked like it was melted into his forearm so that the fabric and the skin were indistinguishable. His arm was roaring red, and the pain seemed all the worse now that he'd seen it. He cursed himself for not being more careful. All the time he'd been spraying the wind was probably bringing some of it back onto this arm it could have been soaked for all he knew as he leaned down to start the fire. It could have been his shirt as much as the wood that caused the flames to go up so fast. How could he had been so stupid?

Sitting up much more carefully this time he looked around the town. It was almost up on him on all sides now and this was what he'd been waiting for. He stood and saw there was a fire going not too far down the hill and he smiled. This had been the couple's car burning, and it was a good size fire already. Even better, he saw that the sky down the mountain was rapidly filling with dark smoke.

"Well done, Sam!" he said feeling that the younger man had been able to get some good spreading fires going.

Joe went to the downhill side of the ceiling and picked up the spray can that was there but found that he couldn't pump the nozzle properly with his injured arm. He cried out in pain as he tried it and dropped the hose. His good arm was killing him and there wasn't enough fire going yet to complete his plan.

Chapter 35

The two women were rigid with fear as they watched the solitary, wary figure move down the centre of the road, his head swivelling all around waiting for some sign that an attack was coming. In his arms, he carried a small box and they could hear the clinking of a few bottles inside as he moved.

Sam could feel their worried eyes on him and it heightened his sense of unease. It made it feel as though something would happen because of how tense everyone was about it, like some ancient self-fulfilling prophesy. He listened keenly against the sound of the wind and the idling engine of the truck; his fear was the sound of the tendrils approaching. He'd seen all too much of how powerful, swift and violent they could be and he didn't want to see another one unless it was dying in flames.

Back up the hill he saw that the fires he'd started with the bottles were growing. He didn't know how long it would take to get going in the way Joe had been counting on but he sure hoped it was sooner than it looked. He turned back to face his own task; there was nothing he could do for Joe now.

Sam was close enough now to hit the tangled mess blocking the road. He set the box down, took out one of the bottles and placed it too on the ground. He lit a match and held it to the rag of sheet in the neck of the bottle and waited for the blue flame to puff into life. The fire took hold of the rag and climbed towards the neck. Sam stood up, planted his feet and threw aiming for dead centre.

His throw was a little off, however, and went too high and dipped down, so much that he thought it wasn't going to hit the wood at all but instead land harmlessly in the snow. Thankfully, the tinkling of shattering glass came at the very bottom of the wall of wood and the fire spread out among the lower limbs as the gas splashed out and caught aflame. As he stood looking at the fire climbing up the wall he saw it was better that he had almost missed. It made much more sense to start the fire at the bottom than in the middle.

He lit another bottle and took a few steps closer this time and aimed for an area about ten feet to the right of the first one and launched it. This time his throw was better, but this meant he didn't get low like the last one, this one hitting about three feet higher from the ground. Still, it would do the trick.

At this moment as he bent to light the next bottle the thought came to his mind, 'Why is this so easy? Why isn't it fighting back?' In that same instant, his ears cocked to the sound they'd all heard earlier on. Fear gripped him, held him firm to the spot. He was looking around but couldn't make out where the sound was coming from.

The loud honk of the truck horn shook him to his senses, and he turned and ran.

"Run Sam!" Sally cried out. "It's coming from the roadblock!" Sam didn't turn to look back, he knew Sally was right and if he hadn't, Susan's screaming of his name would have convinced him just as quickly.

He pumped his legs as fast as he could, feeling the pain in his chest as he gasped in cold air.

"Turn the truck around!" he shouted waving his arms as he ran towards them and seeing as he did that Sally was already doing this.

"Run Sam!" Susan called again as if he was just standing there; the urgency in her voice gave him a boost mentally but his battered body was not up to giving him any more speed or stamina. He buckled slightly at the knees and he could feel himself slowing down, the lack of oxygen pulling at him, telling him to stop.

That was when the horrible fibrous tendrilic noise filled his ears and he felt a sudden hard pain in his left leg as his feet were swept out from under him. He lost all bearing in the fall and landed heavily on his side, gashing his head against the ground.

"Sam!" he made out Susan's hysteric scream and then he felt the grip of the white around his legs and coiling up over his body. He was dazed and winded but he knew he had to get up, that if he didn't this was the end for him. He tried to open his eyes, but they were filled with tears and blurry so he shut them tight again at once.

Snow peppered his face as the rear wheels of the truck skidded to a stop nearby. He heard the doors opening and then noises he couldn't quite make out. He opened his eyes again and could just make out images of movement, what must have been Susan and Sally out trying to pull and smash the killer branches off him.

"Get back in the truck!" he called out in pain. "Get away from here!"

He managed to get his eyes clear, and he saw both women pulling and kicking, both with tears in their eyes and fury in their hearts. It gave him great strength to see how hard they were fighting for him but still he needed them to try to get away and save themselves. He started pulling and snapping at the twigs and tendrils with a renewed strength and anger and to his surprise, he felt the painful crushing of his torso ease a little with the combined efforts of the three of them.

"Wait!" Sally shouted and she broke off from the fight and moved around the truck. At that same instant, a new assault began on his body and Susan shrieked as they pulled and clawed at her too.

"Sally!" Susan called out incredulous that the woman had run off at such a moment as this.

"Take this you filthy killer!" Sally shouted as she came out from the other side of the truck and doused the tendrils beyond Sam and towards the wall in gasoline from one of bottles and then tossed the damp rag she'd already lit up onto it.

The fire whooshed up and almost at once the ends that held Susan and Sam lost their strength and both of them wriggled and dragged themselves free. Sally stamped and jumped at their attackers around the area of the fire and they snapped and cracked and turned to dust all over before pulling back and retreating quickly towards the wall which they noticed now was starting to burn nicely.

"We don't have time to watch this," Sam said pulling at both women's arms. "We need to get in the truck and drive through where the fire is at its most intense in the blockage!"

Susan limped towards the truck but Sally stood where she was looking at the road ahead of them

"Sally!" Sam urged again.

"He's here," she said still staring ahead.

Both Susan and Sam followed the direction of her gaze and sure enough, there at the edge of the forest was the beast made of wood with the man's body, what was once Maul Thorndean's body, staring back at them with a furious and menacing look.

"We need to go now!" Susan shouted and Sam pushed her and helped her into the truck.

"Come on, Sally," Sam said glancing back at Maul. "He doesn't look like he has any plans to help us!" The former tavern keeper stood a moment longer staring before she moved towards the open door of the truck.

As soon as she moved Maul let out a raging howl and moved towards them, not running but moving quickly all the same.

"Quick!" Sam said fumbling for the gun he hadn't even noticed was no longer on him.

Sally jumped in and Sam slammed the door shut behind her and jumped up into the back. He was only in and Sally started the truck moving when Maul slammed hard against it and hooked his thick branch arms over the side. The truck was moving now, back towards Mercy and Sam stamped and pounded at Maul to try to loosen his grip and knock him off but nothing he was doing seemed to have any kind of effect at all.

"Turn!" Maul growled deeply in a voice that was almost like the gruff one he'd owned in his former hermetic life. Sam continued to stamp and kick, taking no notice.

Maul roared in anger once more and one of his arms shot out and landed a heavy punch in Sam's midsection that sent him reeling against the back of the cabin. The women in the front screamed and looked back to try see what was going on.

Sally jammed on the brakes and jumped out in one fluid movement and stood at the side of the truck looking furiously at Maul.

"Maul!" she shouted with tears in her eyes. "What are you doing?"

"Turn," Maul said deeply again without looking her way. He looked at Sam and then at the boxes on the bed of the truck. Sam watched and wished he'd thought of setting Maul on fire instead of trying to kick him off the side. There was nothing he could do now; Maul would have him killed before he could light a single bottle.

Then to the surprise of them all, Maul took up one of the bottles himself. He looked at it carefully like a wild animal inspecting a carcass in the woods appraising it to see if it was edible. Without warning, he took up another bottle and then with a grunted growl smashed them both over his own twiggy bark covered back. He then turned his back to them and jumped down out of the truck.

None of them knew what to do.

Maul began moving back down the road, heading for the blockage. The three of them watched in surprise but also with some great measure of distrust waiting for him to turn and attack again. What started as a shambling gait however very quickly turned in to a run and Maul was off very fast down the road.

"What the hell is he doing?" Sam asked.

"I have no idea," Sally answered.

Maul was nearing the blockage now and they could see the fires Sam had joined up and continuing to spread upwards and outwards.

"He's not going to stop," Sally said just as Maul put his head down and rushed like a football player right into the centre of the wood where the flames burned brightest. Sparks and wood flew in all directions and the sound of the crashing wood filled the air.

"Get back in the truck!" Sam called. "He's punching through for us!"

Sally didn't need to be told twice, she jumped it and let the handbrake off before reengaging the engine and turning the truck around.

"Go, go, go," Sam said pounding on the cab roof. "As fast as you can!"

The truck caromed down the hill gaining speed by the second. Sam had to bend down and hold on tight as it skidded and swerved all over as Sally tried to maintain control. Looking ahead, they saw Maul come back through the wall at another point and now he too was on fire. Howling like a wild animal, he looked at them one last time and then went running through the woods back towards Mercy, setting branches and twigs alight as he went.

"Hold on tight!" Sally shouted as they bore down on the now inferno-like blockage in the road.

Sam dropped behind the cabin now and then with horror his eyes fell on the still unused bottles filled with gasoline. It was too late for him to do anything about it now, all he could do was hope they didn't catch fire or explode and he turned away and covered himself as best he could in case they did.

Chapter 36

Joe took the hose of the gas can in his weaker but functioning left hand, leaving the can itself on the surface. He sprayed a mist out into the closest trees and then took a step back. He would not be able to get much done like this with only one arm. The injured one throbbed and stung now with a strange kind of pain he'd never felt before. He looked to his pile of ammunition in the centre of the roof ruefully.

The fire he had going was probably not going to do the job as things stood. He would have to do better, and fast. Rushing to the gasoline, he took up three bottles in his good arm and carried them to the edge. After setting them down right side up he struck a new match — not an easy thing to do with only one hand — and lit them all at once. Then he lifted them one at a time, arched his left arm back and tossed the flaming bottles as far as he could.

The first one landed against the trunk of a tree about fifteen feet away and Joe was glad to see flames burst out over it. The second one sailed through some branches and then landed with a hiss in the snow.

"Goddamnit, it would have been easier to hit than miss with all the trees here!" he shouted angrily. He plucked up the next and threw without aiming and this time it hit a y-section where the trunk separated and two small fires started. That was something at least. Looking around, he could see that there were eight distinct fires going at the moment in the vicinity of the town but he didn't know if it was enough to engulf the whole place later on. Down the mountain he could see that the fires Sam had started were growing and the amount of smoke told a job well done. Perhaps it would have been better if Sam had been the one to stay behind and try to kill this thing; he probably wouldn't have set himself on fire and stacked the deck further against himself like Joe had.

No, now was not the time for negative thinking; there was a job still to be done. He wasn't in the shape he'd hoped to be doing it and he wouldn't be as effective as he'd envisioned either but he could still do it!

The trees were practically all white now and bending in towards all the buildings in Mercy in the same way as they had at Maul's house. Joe ran to the spray can and pumped it once more before using his single hand again to spray a new long mist over the trees to the back of the building. He lit a new rag up and dropped it this time rather than placing it and watched the fire crackle up in the brush below and start spreading into the trees around.

"You can do this!" he said.

Glancing around he saw it might take a while for the fires to reach where he'd left the explosives. He could be dead by the time those went off. It wasn't so important that he be alive when this happened, but he sure would like to be around for it. He supposed for now all he could do was keep tossing out these bottles into areas that weren't on fire yet and hope they caught and started to spread. Again, he cursed his stupidity in hindering himself. He knew he could have thrown almost double the distance he was getting now if his right arm was still serviceable.

He went on a series of runs then from the middle back to the edges all around, placing the full bottles and the cans of gas around the rim of the tavern roof. Then lighting one of the rags he started a circle of what he'd just done lighting up a bottle and throwing it into the trees in all directions. Some lit up well, and he was gladdened to see the same kind of burst of flames that had hurt his arm. Others landed flat in the snow and petered out, but he had to take the victories where they came now.

Joe was almost out of bottles by this point and that was when over the noise of the fires he heard a new noise in the air. It was low level, but he knew at once what it was. It was the trees coming for him. They'd put up with enough of his fighting back and they would put an end to it.

"Come on you bastard!" he shouted out in fury, pulling one of the heavy gas cans back to the doorway. He opened the lid and let the can fall on its side. Pungent gasoline slicked its way down the stairs back into the tavern. Joe watched until he saw it had reached the bottom and then touched a flaming rag to it and watched as the fires rushed downstairs cutting off his only means of escape.

Joe also knew, of course, that the tavern would go fully up on fire too and would add to the intensity and power of the surrounding fires. He hoped dearly that this would be the last impetus it would need to really get spreading all over the mountainside. The noises of the gripping fingers of the white death gathered around the building and Joe stood up to face it.

Looking out he could not see where it was coming from but he thought he could tell the direction. His eyes bore into the trees waiting for it to arrive. He'd done all he could; it seemed as if this was to be his time.

Then a new noise came to his ears, and he turned and looked toward this interruption. A growling hulking mass erupted from the trees from the other end of Mercy. Joe saw with great surprise that it was Maul and not only that, he was on fire himself.

Maul moved and cut through more of the dead trees and Joe saw he was spreading fire wherever he went. The creature was stumbling and tottering and it wailed in what Joe felt must have been pain. He felt great pity for the sight he was seeing, of what the once powerful and fearless man had become. It was a good thing that he would soon be wiped from this earth, but it was a shame it wasn't in a way more fitting to the way he'd lived his life.

Chapter 37

Susan's sustained scream was drowned out by the shattering of limbs and the crackling roar of fire as the truck smashed into the barrier blocking their way to Emerson. Sparks and glowing embers and pieces of broken twig and branch rained down on the truck. Sam, feeling his ear burnt by one of these suddenly had a new fear and he dived on top of the gasoline pile covering it as best he could lest one of these small pieces should start the fire and explosions he'd been so worried about.

Maul had weakened the wall enough that the truck was making good progress and only slowing a little as it piled through. Sam could hear the hissing of the fire in the trees like they were wailing out in pain. The heat was intense, and he didn't dare look up for fear of what might happen to his eyes. Whipping noises came from above his head and there was constant thudding and banging against the sides and roof of the ruck. Even without seeing Sam knew that these were the flailing tendrils fighting against dying or at the very least trying to take the occupants of this dashing vehicle along with them.

It may have only been three seconds since they entered the firestorm but to Sam it felt like at least a minute already. He hadn't expected the wall to be so thick but at the speed it felt they were going, even with the slight slowdown, they must have already covered over one hundred yards. How deep could it be!

Susan was still screaming and Sally was shouting something, one long word it seemed that he could not make out. How much longer could it be before they were through? Was there an end to this?

A gust of cold air whipped over his skin and suddenly all the heat and noise rapidly diminished. Opening his eyes he saw the clear sky above him and he sat up to look around and fresh wind buffeted his face, snow tapping his cheek. He looked behind them, had they made it?

They were clear! He couldn't believe it but at the same time a huge sigh of relief drew from him and he sat back on the bed of the truck, looking at the flaming forest they were now happily leaving behind them. Susan had stopped screaming and now both she and Sally were cheering and hooting happily in the front seats.

"We did it!" Sally shouted pumping her fist in the air out the window.

"Good driving!" Sam shouted not moving from the spot he'd slumped in to rest.

"Are you alright back there?" Susan called back to him.

"I'm fine," he answered but then his gut contracted at the sound that came to his ears. It was far off, but he knew at once what it was. "Sally, if you can get this thing to go any faster do it now!"

"What is it?" Susan asked trying to look behind. Sally didn't ask but just made sure she was pressing the accelerator pedal down as far as it would go.

"Hold on, Sam," she called back. "This road is thick with snow and things might get a little slippy!"

Sam didn't answer, he was looking behind them waiting for what he knew was coming. The trees on either side of the road were spread out now, getting farther away from the road as they descended and the only white that showed on these was that of the snowfall of recent weeks. The attack would be coming from the forest they had left behind and if for whatever reason it couldn't catch them, they would be free and clean. Everything was on a knife-edge.

From the ever-spreading fire, thicker limbs than before crawled out like snakes and rushed down the centre of the road after them. For one beautiful moment, when all the limbs joined and came at them as one, it looked to Sam like they only matched the speed of the car and wouldn't be able to close the gap between them. It was, however, only a moment, and he looked on with dismay as the thundering wood gathered speed in its wild pursuit.

Looking down at the last of the gasoline he didn't see that it would be of much use in fending off this last attack. He looked to the side of the cabin where Susan would be sitting and then saw her reflection in the side mirror. She was looking ahead with that same fearful pained look on her face he'd seen earlier and his heart ached to think she was in such danger. He looked at the bottles and gas drums again and he knew what he would have to do. If he couldn't stop it with the little amount of firepower he could throw in one go, he might be able to stop it by severing the head with all the firepower at once. He would have to work fast!

He pulled the gas cans as far to back of the truck bed as he could and the looked around for something to use to stuff the openings like they had the bottles earlier. There was nothing around but a length of old coiled rope and he picked it to see how thick it was. Sam could tell at once that it was not thick enough to fill the necks and stay in place but he had a new purpose for it at once. He ran it through the handles of all the drums and pulled them tight together before tying as good a knot as he could to hold them all in place. Then he unscrewed all the lids, pulled off his jacket and using his pocket knife tore off some shreds to dip in gas and stuff the necks.

Glancing back, he saw he wasn't going to have enough time to get to all of them so he left it at the first two and poured some more gas over the top and sides of all the drums to coat them. He tied the other end of the rope around his waist and pulled hard, hurting his sides and he tugged the gas drums towards his back.

"Sally!" he shouted.

"Yeah?"

"Whatever happens, just keep going alright?"

"What are you doing?"

"Sam?" Susan called out in worry. He looked to her side and met her eyes in the side mirror. She looked so frightened it killed him.

"I love you, Susan," he called to her. "I'm sorry I took so long to let you know how I felt!" He knew she couldn't feel the same way on such a short time together so he kicked the flap at the end of the truck down and saw the limbs were just about to catch up with them, tendril fingers reaching to the back of the truck.

"Sam!" Susan screamed as he set fire to the bottles in the box, picked it up and jumped into the maw of the white death.

The limbs gripped around him at once and as the gas spread and a huge fireball exploded out in all directions as the gas cans went up along with the last of the bottles.

The truck sped on, the limbs stopped now and the distance growing and growing. Sally looked out through the side window and tears rolled down her cheeks. Susan screamed once and then fell sobbing into her own knees. The truck kept on going down the mountain towards the valley, no longer pursued.

Chapter 38

Joe moved the edge of the roof closest to where Maul was to call out to him.

"Maul," he shouted, but this made no impression on the creature powering through the trees. Joe shouted his name once more, but the howling whining of the approaching tendril grew louder and coupled with the roar of the fires and Maul's own noise he still couldn't be heard.

Joe looked around in despair for something that might be loud enough to get his attention and then the answer came to him. He pulled his gun from its holster.

"Not much louder than a gun shot!" he said as he squeezed off the shot into the air.

This time Maul did stop, and he looked over and Joe met his eyes.

"You're still in there," Joe murmured with certainty now. "Go into the houses and set them on fire!" he shouted to Maul. The woody abomination made no indication that he understood what was said to him and went on rampaging through the trees.

"Fuck!" Joe shouted in frustration but then as he watched he saw how much fire there was and understood that Maul was, intentionally or not, joining up the lesser fires to add the power of the larger ones to them.

Joe bent and lit two more bottles as he saw the tendril come through the branches towards him. He stood his ground and shouted at the impending limbs.

"Not without a fight you bastards!" And even with all that was going on he got the sense of how insane a situation he'd found himself in and he laughed out loud at the surrealistic nature of it all.

The first of the limbs grappled with his legs and pulled them out from under him. Joe fell flat on his back but he'd seen it coming at the last moment and managed not to drop the bottles and only spilled a little. He sat up as quick as he went down and smashed one of the bottles over the tendrils and watched the flames spread. There was a whining noise like pain and it was very satisfying for him to hear at that moment. More tendrils were coming and just as those got to him he smashed the second bottle over them. Fire spread over them and they too made pained noises and Joe felt the power of them lessen and they cracked and fell apart in the fire. Pulling himself back, he managed to get clear and stand up once more.

Down below he saw Maul barge through where the limbs had been coming from and he heard terrible crashing and shouting and more of this whining agonized sounds.

"Go get em' Maul!" he shouted and in his eagerness Joe picked up one of the half-filled drums and ran to the edge and tossed it into the trees that were already alight.

There was a loud hiss and then a huge fireball rose up and hot air blew back over Joe. He covered his face but when he looked back, he was delighted to see that this little stunt had spread the fire to a new section that had been untouched so far.

He knew his time was almost up now and this was about all he would be able to do, so he picked up another drum, heavier and fuller this time, and spinning like a hammer thrower tossed it out into those same trees. He jumped back this time knowing that the explosion would be bigger with the fuller drum.

The result was he hoped and when he could see properly, he saw the new patch of fire had doubled in size already. The joy at this soured quickly then when he realised this was the extent of what he would be able to do from the roof now. There were a couple of drums left and a few bottles but he wouldn't be able to do anything with them with only his weak arm.

Maul erupted once more from the forest and now he was completely engulfed in flames and almost unable to keep on walking. Joe looked down at him and then around at the forest. Fire was raging all over and it was spreading. Down the mountain was ablaze and now Mercy was getting there. He thought he'd done enough; he thought they had done enough. Everyone played their part, even Maul.

"What a time for the town to finally all come together," Joe said and the smile with this broke and tears began to run down his cheeks with the final acceptance of his fate.

As if on cue a section of the roof behind him collapsed under the fire and he fell over and then slid to the edge and over onto the street. He landed in a heavy bank of snow but it was soaked from the heat and from where he lay he could see that there was a thin stream running down the centre of the street from all the melting snow everywhere.

Joe's arm hurt more than ever now and he rolled over and looked up the street through blurry eyes. As he did, the fiery visage of Maul Thorndean came flailing from between the buildings onto the main road. He looked at Joe for a moment and then ran on smashing his way into Susan Bloom's old place.

Smoke blew at Joe and he coughed and felt a huge pain in his ribs. It was at that moment he knew for the first time that his legs were no longer working. He couldn't feel any pain that might explain this but it was the case all the same. He lay back on the cold snow and with the sound of Maul smashing up and laying fire to the buildings of the town, looked up at the sky, every now and then seeing the black blanket and the twinkling stars and wondering if anyone had made it off the mountain that night.

Chapter 39

When Sally got to Emerson in the middle of the night, she passed dozens of people standing in the streets outside their houses all staring up and pointing at the inexplicable sight of the forest on fire in the middle of one of the coldest and snowiest months the state had ever seen.

No one paid any attention as she slowly drove along the streets with the last bottle of gasoline rolling about in the bed of the truck. Susan was asleep, she'd cried so much at Sam's passing and coupled with her own pain it was all too much for her. Sally thought her body had probably shut down as a defence mechanism. She was breathing steadily so Sally wasn't too worried but she wanted to get her to the medical centre all the same.

It was unlikely to be open now, so she knew she would have to make a pass at the police station first. This was the part she didn't want to have to go through. To be the person to try to tell the world what had happened up there would be very tough and draining on her.

The handbrake creaked loudly as Sally stopped outside the station. An officer on duty looked out lazily through the glass door most likely hoping this was not something he was going to have to deal with. Sally looked back and was sure he wouldn't be able to make out her face from this distance. She looked at Susan and then back to the station.

Was there really any point in going in there? What would they do except ask hundreds of questions or worse still, laugh her out of there. She was sure she could take care of Susan in the meantime until they could get to another town.

If they went away, Sally could write a letter, put down everything she knew about what had happened to Mercy and everyone in it. She could tell about Jarrod and Ava, the heroics of Sam and Joe. She could tell them about Maul and warn them what to be on the lookout for. She could say all this and not be interrupted by one question, one laugh, or one raised eyebrow.

They would want to talk to them both, and in time Sally was sure that was what they would do. But for now, for tonight and until Susan was better, it was more appealing to keep on going, to get away from the present. The snow was still falling but lighter here in the valley, not so much of a covering on the ground. It looked like a very nice place to live, but so too had Mercy once.

Perhaps somewhere with more sun, she thought as she pulled the truck back out into the road. The police offer looking back down then at his newspaper or some other reading material.

"It will come out better on paper," she said. "Everyone will come out better on paper."

The End

Sign up for free books and newsletter/new releases here[1]
Learn more about European P. Douglas here[2]

---

1.   http://eepurl.com/bWwroj

2.   https://www.amazon.com/European-P.-Douglas/e/B008OEQM9W/
ref=dp_byline_cont_ebooks_1

Made in the
USA
Monee, IL